In Life, In Love, In Rodeo there are always . . .

Crucial Turns

. . . to survive and win

Judy (Meyer) Smith

A special thanks to
Phil Roth
for the metalwork
on the cover

PROLOGUE

Traditions be damned—

I thought to myself,
Not in this house—
Not in my family—

It is the fourth Thursday of November, declared in 1863 as a day to be thankful, a day of giving, and a sacred day of tradition. Since I was born, the days of Thanksgiving and Christmas have been commercialized, and so, I'll say it again—*traditions be damned—not in this house—not in my family.*

The smell of turkey and the sound of football fill the house. I wait for silence as I sit in my chair and rock to and fro. I hear squeaks from joints that are old. These *squeaks* have soothed all the babies born into this family, save one. I hear footsteps and I smell a baby, clean and powder fresh. I take the child, and he finds my breast just as the others come into the room.

The TV has been turned off, the dishes dried and put away. There are seats for all the adults, and the children surround me as they find their place in the circle. On my right and on my left are the oldest and the tallest—from them, the children go in steps to the youngest and smallest who stands directly across from me. The hands of the oldest and the tallest boys are on the finials of my chair and I hear them whisper, "It's time. Ask the question." Their words are repeated around the circle until the two youngest come to stand in front of me. They gently place a book in my lap and ask if I will read them a story.

1

When I rock forward, the book starts to slide, and I catch it with my right hand. My chair stops at the tip of its rails. The baby is safe in the crook of my left arm. I think to myself that I don't need to open the book to recall my adventures. I remember *each*—and *every* word I had written. I look at the children and I smile. I tell them to "Sit down because this is a very long story. It may take me until Christmas to finish telling." Each evening I share some of my life. When the children have grown up—and become adults—my hope is that the boys will have learned to be good and kind—tolerant and respectful men. They will have heard the story of my life in its entirety.

So, I begin to tell my tale—

a story about myself—

a girl by the name of Chris—

who grew and matured in the summers of 71 and 2.

My story begins in the middle of the night—

Chapter 1

Inside the bus station an old man stood behind the ticket counter. He lifted his eyes to acknowledge my presence, but neither of us spoke. I leaned against the crumbling block wall to wait for my next bus. The following day another bus would take me home and end my travels.

On the wall was a map. Every bus station in the country had one, and so did my parents. My mother had tied a knot at the end of a spool of thread. Through that knot, she stuck a pin into Oklahoma City. Each time we would talk, she would stick another pin, or two into the map. When the pins were secure, she would unwind thread and wrap it around each pin to show my path. She had nearly unwound the entire spool of thread tracing my travels. I had gone east then west and north to south, again, and again, crisscrossing the country. I could say that I knew my country very well and I could truly call it mine. I had traveled nearly fifty thousand miles.

That night when my bus arrived, the old man locked his door, and no doubt went home and slept in his bed. At least that night, I had been a reason for him to stay late I told myself. I found it unsettling, and my mother didn't like it when I had to stand outside to wait for the next bus alone—in the middle of the night. Those were the nights I had no place to seek cover if the weather turned bad.

I was ready to ditch my backpack, tired of resembling the pack mules at the Grand Canyon. For months I had carried all my possessions on my back, and some people called me homeless. Others thought I had run away, but I had a home and I would be there soon. I was sure of that.

The next driver allowed me to board the bus early. I looked down the aisle and saw sleepers sprawled over two or three seats. Feet hung into the aisle or stretched across it, an obstacle course to my favorite seat at the back of the bus. I dropped my backpack at the first row of seats and sat behind the driver.

I took advantage of his light and mirror to look at myself. My washed out, faded and fraying jeans were stuffed into my boots. An army shirt, brown and green in color, covered the t-shirt I'd worn inside out for weeks. When I got home, I'd have to get my hair cut because Mom wouldn't stand for it looking the way it did that day and I knew she'd replace all my clothes. I had given away my winter coat. It was too heavy to wear, too bulky to pack, and unnecessary in May.

Mom would have said I looked like one of those *hippies* she had seen on the news, but I looked healthy and I felt good.

As the bus pulled away from the curb, I remembered angry words from years before. "Why? Why should I? Tell me why!" Anger radiated throughout my body. I'd been having more trouble with my vision, and the tension over my eyesight had escalated when my mother tried to make decisions for me. I remembered my dad's hand on my back. He guided me away from my mother and demanded that I sit down. His voice was low and composed when he said, "Take a deep breath and let go of the anger." I don't know why it took so long for my dad to say what he meant, or for me to realize he was right in saying what he did. I closed my eyes and slept that night listening to the sound of bus wheels.

Yes—I had been angry, but I knew my parents *loved* me. I embarked on my journey to learn about the country I was born and raised in—the one my father died serving. Now that I knew it *inside out* and *backwards*, I could truly call it mine.

When I woke up, it was morning and the driver told me, "Don't miss the next bus."

I smiled and told him not to worry, "I plan to be home for Mother's Day."

When the bus moved away, I looked at a banner strung across the street. Santa Rosa was having their rodeo that weekend. As a family, we had always gone to the National Finals. The cowboys there were the best. The Finals in Oklahoma City were at the end of the school

4

term for my mother. She had been a teacher for years. Mom said that my father had *dreamed* of winning a gold buckle before he died—so we always went—mom, dad, and me.

I had hours to wait for my next bus, so I walked in the direction of the rodeo, thankful that I was not captive to daily body counts and news clips every night. When I passed the post office I thought I should send my journal home—it was nearly full—but I decided instead that if I kept it with me, I could share it with my parents when I arrived.

I stopped to read a rodeo poster. A truck stopped beside me, and the driver offered me a ride to the rodeo. He had his family in the cab with him, which made me feel safe, so I stepped onto the bumper and over the tailgate. I got to the front of the truck bed and sat on a green cooler. The back window was gone, and I talked to the couple, no older than myself. The driver said that he'd just gotten back from a tour in Vietnam. President Nixon was in the middle of his first term and Vietnam was the news of the day. Their young son stood on the seat between them and smiled at me. I wondered if this could have been my life, if my father had not died in Korea before I was born.

I waved as the truck disappeared on the gentle hillside north of the arena where the rodeo was to take place. Camping there would have been fun. Kids were everywhere, and many had a horse. There was a mist rising from the shovel truck as the sun climbed higher in the sky. The stinking load would fertilize some field or garden before the rodeo began.

I walked through the unattended gate and entered a new world. I moved a bale of hay to hide my belongings. I thought this would be better than leaving them exposed in a corner of the bus station. I didn't have a tent, and since I had to catch another bus to get home after dinner, I didn't try to find space in the campground. I'd be gone before dark anyway.

I stood with my feet some distance apart. My thumbs were hooked inside my back pockets and I watched a horse outside the arena. I heard a stern voice behind me say, "Move to one side. You'll get hurt if you stand there." I turned to see a cowboy on an almost white horse. His voice was unyielding. He was clean-shaven, but I couldn't see his eyes shaded by the brim of his hat. I backed into the fence, so he could pass by. "Stay out of trouble," he said, clearly irritated at something or someone. When he had moved past, I climbed a section of fence

5

boards to get a better look inside the arena. "Get down from there!" This time the man was angry. He walked up to me, his horse following, and I dropped to the ground. He looked down at me. He had to be six foot and something, and I was only five-five. "I wouldn't want you to get hurt." This time his voice sounded kind, and he grinned. I watched him open and then close the gate I'd been sitting on and he rode away.

The water truck came and spread water in the arena. For a short time, I wouldn't have to breathe dust. I only realized I'd missed my bus when I heard the call for riders to gather in the northeast corner. It was already seven and growing dark. I had not paid attention to people arriving for the rodeo. The grandstand was full, and so was the fence where I sat. Riders of all ages who could sit a horse had been lining up outside the arena to be in the Grand Entry—every rodeo started with one. Finally, a rider entered the arena holding the American Flag. She was surrounded by her Color Guard. Behind them trailed the remaining riders—two and three abreast, they circled the edge of the arena in well-ordered fashion. The gate from which they had entered closed after the last rider was inside. That was the signal for the girls with colored flags to drop out of line and take their assigned positions in the center of the arena. An impressively dressed cowboy urged his horse to close the gap the girls left, and the remaining riders moved with him.

As spectators, we watched as the girl carrying the national flag and the man on his white horse broke formation. They picked up the pace and led the riders, in and out, serpentine fashion around the stationary horses with their colored flags. As the last rider at the end of the long line passed by the girl with her flag, she turned her horse in a complete circle and spurred them to a gallop to re-join the parade. This happened seven times more.

The girls with their flags waited until all the riders left the arena. The stars and stripes, flanked by the color guard, returned to the arena's center. The colored flags were all three foot by five and attached to eight-foot wooden poles. The poles rested in boot cups and a hand—held the pole just beneath the flag. At home, I knew girls that were part of a drill team who performed at rodeos all over the state with their flags.

The crowd clapped loudly as I recognized the man who had been disgruntled with me. He approached the line of girls in the center of the arena on his horse. "Joe Engelmann," the announcer's voice boomed, was from Horse Springs, New Mexico.

Mr. Engelmann had changed his clothes and I watched him lift his black hat by its crown and hold it high as he acknowledged the crowd. He was good looking. He was smiling, and he turned toward the horse beside him and the American flag. I saw the girl stand in her stirrups, and on cue—a spoken word or pressure from her leg—the horse jumped to a gallop. Fully open, the flag flew by all of us. It was more than twice the size of the others. We stood as it approached—on the fence boards, in stirrups, on the ground—we were all at attention. Hats came off heads—everyone was respectful. The girl with her flag completed a circle around the arena. Her horse slid to a stop, dirt sprayed, and they faced Mr. Engelmann again. The flag covered her hand, she moved the pole, and the flag straightened itself. She wore white gloves. Joe's hat and his right hand covered his heart. I felt my own heart beating beneath my hand as I joined in with the words, "I pledge Allegiance. . ." The words resonated in that small valley. I thought about my father and whispered a silent prayer for the souls lost in war. You could have heard a pin drop.

I thought back to a fort outside Baltimore where they showed a film about the War of 1812 and the writing of the National Anthem. When the film was over, they opened a twelve-foot-tall curtain to expose a wall of glass nearly three times as tall as I. I remembered a billowing flag at the center of Fort McHenry. I'm sure it was the same as when Keyes first penned his words to paper.

Now, a single spot of light focused on the flag. My voice trembled as I mouthed the words, "O, say, can you see. . ." I could hear the horses and see the flag flying around the arena one last time as we sang.

Switches were flipped and lights came on. The rodeo had begun, and when it ended, the crowd left, but not the cowboys. There was never enough time for all competitors to compete during the performance, so men waited their turn. When the slack had finished, the lights went out, the arena was quiet, and I slept on a stack of hay bales. When I closed my eyes that night, I remembered thinking that there would be another bus the next day. The only problem was, I wasn't going to make it home by Mother's Day, but I'd be home on Monday. Mom would have to settle for that because I had tried.

Chapter 2

In the morning, before anyone else was in the arena, I stuffed my backpack between two hay bales. I climbed the nearby fence and a gentle breeze brought the scent of Old Spice to my nose. My body stiffened as I recognized Mr. Engelmann's voice behind me. He seemed unperturbed by me that day. "You gonna watch them all day? The rodeo won't start until two, but there's a parade at ten." I waited to see what he would say next. "I didn't say you did anything wrong."

I turned slowly to see that his hat was pushed back to expose dark brown hair. Yesterday I'd seen his hair cut short and shaved at the neck. Today, he carried a second hat and two apples. He reached up and plunked the hat on my head, "I thought you could use some shade, if you're going to sit fence all day." He handed me an apple and took a bite out of the other. I pulled at my shirt to polish the apple. "Did you know some people are born with rodeo in their blood?"

I still hadn't said a word and I figured that I should say something, or he might think I was dumb, so I said, "Thanks, Mr. Engelmann." I tried to make the hat fit my head, but it was too big. "You're the stock contractor. Do you ride too?" He watched me as he climbed the fence. His arm brushed mine as he stepped over the top two boards and sat beside me, our heels were hooked beneath us on the edge of a board.

"I've won buckles and broke a few bones like everybody." He never looked away from me, "Why don't you just call me Joe, everyone else does." He continued to talk as we watched what went on inside the arena. "I don't actively compete anymore, but do you? Do you live nearby?" he asked without seeming to take a breath. "You're too scrawny to pull a steer down, but you could learn to rope."

9

Joe must have thought I was a boy because he didn't say anything about barrel racing. That was the only event where girls could compete. The female trick riders were just coming in and I lost myself in daydreams. I knew how to ride, and I was sure I could carry a flag and do the barrels. I didn't think I'd ever have the nerve to do a fender ride. The girls rode with a single foot in the stirrup or special strap that hung off the side of their saddles. Sometimes they faced backwards. I was impressed when I saw a girl stand on the saddle of a galloping horse with her hands raised to the sky doing a hippodrome stand. I wondered how the horses knew what the riders wanted them to do. The girls practiced, and I couldn't take my eyes off them.

I don't know how long Joe watched from beside me. I didn't hear or feel him leave the fence we had shared. When the girls were finished, two of them—who turned out to be sisters—came over and showed me the special straps and modifications they had made to their windswept saddle. They said the barrel swept back, so they couldn't fall. The horn was taller for doing their tricks, but they liked it for doing barrels too. They slipped the toes of their shoes into loops created by their straps. Their toes pointed to the ground—heels latched into place with a click. That secured them to their saddles they said—and to their horses. For other tricks they would kneel and as they stood up, the girls would drop the reins. The horses would feel weight shift from their backs to their shoulders. With the voice command "hup," they would break into a canter. The sisters rode off for the parade.

I stayed where I was because things were still happening inside the arena. Girls raced around the barrels. Calves ran from ropers. Nobody practiced on any of the bucking stock. When the water truck came, everyone left. It was the signal to get ready because spectators had begun to arrive.

After the rodeo, I slid my hands into my pockets and came up with my folded-up wad of bus tickets, some lint but no cash. I pulled my belt tighter. I'd have to get to a bank for a wire transfer, and they wouldn't be open until Monday. Mr. Engelmann must have been watching. He approached and quietly asked when I'd eaten last. He put his hand on my shoulder, and I was afraid to move. "What's it to you?" I said, not lifting my eyes from the ground in front of me.

"You look a little hungry and a whole lot broke."

I'd felt Dad's hand tighten on my shoulder many times growing up. Especially when I'd done something—I knew I shouldn't have. I remembered my bus, I kicked at the ground and dirt flew. My voice was antagonistic when I said, "So, what if I am?" And just that quickly I had forgotten my bus again. But I had time to get to the bus, and if I did, I'd be home on Monday morning, but that's not what happened. The pressure on my shoulder was gone. I watched Mr. Engelmann take some bills from his leather money clip. I told him I didn't need his money and tried to walk away.

He moved beside me, and then he stepped in front of me. Joe Engelmann blindsided me and I ran into him. He looked down at me as he folded some bills in half and in half again. "Get something to eat," he said as he shoved the money into my shirt pocket. "I saw you tighten your belt, and an apple a day isn't enough for a growin' boy." He was annoyed with me, I could hear it in his voice, and then he walked away without another word. I watched him shake his head, and I thought to myself, he actually thinks I'm a boy.

I pulled the bills from my pocket—four singles and a ten. A cold chill went down my spine, a mistake I was sure. I should eat, I knew that, but I couldn't, not then. I had to find a journal, and the ten was just enough to get me one that was leather bound. I had run out of room in the one I'd been writing in the night before, and now I was afraid I'd forget something.

I never thought about the bus again. I forgot about Oklahoma, my parents and home. I needed to record every movement—every sound—even the smell of the shovel truck. I had sat close enough to hear the Chute Boss call for the next rider up. He knew the stock and was responsible for getting the right man onto the right animal at the right time. He played games with people's names. I remembered a redheaded cowboy. The Chute Boss had yelled something about him being "loose in the head," but nobody seemed to get angry with him. Mike must have been the man's name because I heard somebody ask if "Mike-ee" could come out and play.

Calves ran and ropers caught them. Cowboys transferred from their horse to steers to bring them the ground as quickly as they could. There were boxes on either side of the chute that released calves and steers. A twine barrier in front of the cowboy's horse gave the calf or steer a head start. Cowboys lost time if they broke the twine by coming out of the box early. Girls backed into the boxes to build

11

momentum for their sprint around the barrels. Each barrel knocked over added five seconds to their time.

I left the rodeo grounds with carloads of people moving in the direction of downtown. I hoped to find another journal, but if not, I'd have settled for a loose-leaf binder filled with paper and transfer my thoughts later. I found a stationery store and the shopkeeper beamed when I chose a leather-tooled journal from her showcase. I pocketed the fifty-cent piece I received as change and I was glad when the woman offered me a ride back to the fairgrounds. It was getting dark and she said that she'd feel better if she dropped me off at the campground.

Everything was quiet at the rodeo grounds. There was nobody to interrupt my thoughts that evening. The bales of hay around my backpack had decreased. I counted ten and pulled three off the pile to make a bed. I smelled alfalfa as I sat down to write. When I could no longer see my words, I slid my pen into the piece of leather made for it. I closed the cover and slipped the journal between my jeans and t-shirt. It had been two long days and one very short night. The calves beside me were already asleep and I slept soundly and dreamed about what might happen the next day.

Chapter 3

I was just coming out of a deep sleep when I heard voices. I couldn't tell who was talking at first, and then I recognized Mr. Engelmann's voice, "You gonna sleep the day away?" I felt something push against the thinning leather of my boots, first one, and then the other.

I pulled the hat Joe had given me the day before off my face and asked, "What time is it?"

"S'ven-fifteen, and I'd like to feed my stock with your mattress."

I eased the hat onto my head and moved my backpack. I stood and straightened my outer shirt and tucked it into my jeans to make sure my journal was secure. "I can help with that, Mr. Engelmann."

"Didn't I tell you yesterday to call me Joe? Everyone else does."

"Yes sir. I'll remember . . . Joe," I said, as Joe picked up a bale of alfalfa and rested it on the fence's top board. I straddled the same board and cut each piece of twine with one pull of my knife. I put the knife away and tossed chunks of hay to the animals.

"Gotta be a boy," Joe muttered. "I'm not stupid." I saw Joe turn to face another cowboy. "Don't say it." Joe placed another bale on the fence for me, and then he lifted his hat as he pulled a short comb from his pocket and ran it through his wavy hair. "I knew he had a reputation for causing trouble when I hired him, Mason."

"Don't let Tina hear you call me that. You know well enough, my name's Bob."

"And how're you and your new bride getting along?" Joe asked.

"I'm an old married man now. It's been a year since the wedding."

"I know but when I see her look at you—I'd swear you were still honey moonin'."

"Why don't you offer and pay that kid for day work?"

The banter between the two men had changed to center on me, and I listened closely. I hesitated to look at them, but when Bob Mason said, I'd think you'd get tired of gathering up destitute drifters when you don't know anything about them—I did.

"And you want me to hire another one. What do you think I am— a magnet for stray souls?"

"You knew what you were doing when you hired Tom and every other vagrant on your payroll," Bob said as he walked away.

"The sisters said the kid's name was Chris," Joe called out and I turned my head to look at the two men.

"So—What is Chris?" Bob Mason asked, "Tina says Chris is a girl."

"Can't be," Joe shook his head. "A good parent wouldn't let a girl that age run around on her own. The kid is a boy. How old, I'm not sure, but a boy!" Bob Mason walked away laughing.

When I came off the third fence, my knees buckled beneath me and Joe caught my wrists as I sat in the dirt. Joe pulled me to my feet and reached for my journal, its cover was open. He read my name, "This time you're going to eat, Chris Latham." He grabbed at the twine, and taking me by the elbow, walked me to where the locals were serving breakfast. "Save a chair for me and we'll talk." He placed my journal beside me, dropped the twine into a trash barrel, and then approached the sheriff. He was collecting the money from anyone who wanted to eat breakfast. "See the boy over there?" I heard Joe ask the sheriff. He turned to watch me pick up my journal.

The sheriff shook his head. I didn't think he could tell Joe anything about me. Joe told him my name. He made a gesture with his hand indicating how tall I was. I'm sure he calculated my weight when he pulled me to my feet. The sheriff listened to Joe tell him that I had brown hair, and hazel eyes. I'm sure Joe couldn't tell him how long I'd been traveling. I hoped he didn't say I was taking drugs. He might have called me a *hippie,* but I wasn't sure. Joe and the sheriff were both studying me when I looked up from my journal. The sheriff said "Educated," as he wrote in a notepad beside him. I wrote down their conversation in my own journal.

The sheriff said he would take me with him when he was finished collecting money, and I looked at them with my mouth open. Joe shook his head and told him I hadn't done anything wrong. He said he'd feed and offer me steady work. Joe didn't think I'd turn him down. He told the sheriff that if he came across a runaway of my description or name, he could be reached in Horse Springs at the Engelmann Ranch.

I took a deep breath, and closed my journal when Joe brought food and drink to our table. Plates of pancakes and sausage links were stacked high. I thought I saw his eyes close briefly as he removed his hat. "I did eat fry bread with honey last night," I told him.

"Beans would've been better." Joe divided the food and drink between us. "If I hire you, can you work past September, or will you return to school?" I shook my head and told Joe that if this were a real job, I might not go back.

Joe kept referring to me as a boy, and I didn't correct him. I didn't want to get fired before I had the chance to prove myself. After the stock was watered, Joe showered, shaved, and told me he had somewhere to go. He said I could take a dry towel from the line and use his toiletries to clean up at the showers. I had my own soap and shampoo, so I showered, even though all my clothes were dirty.

When he returned, I asked where the others were that I'd seen the day before. "They work for you, don't they?"

"Immature idiots," he said and then just as quickly his anger abated. He explained Texas Tom guzzled too much beer the night before. There was an argument with Nate that resulted in blows. John tried to break it up and finally George and my Chute Boss stepped in. When the Sheriff got them separated, he jailed everyone. "Behind the chutes," Joe said, "We police ourselves, but in town you go to jail, no questions asked."

I shuddered. Were the men working for Joe all drunks? These men were adults, but I supposed even they behaved badly at times. I came down to the arena to watch him move stock around for the afternoon's performance. Joe called out to cowboys to help him with the calves. He saw me and told me to go open a gate. When the gate latched, I asked, "What's next?"

"Meet me by the bucking chutes but don't get in the way."

15

I was going to protest and then I remembered cowboys with the toes of their boots between the fence boards, hanging over the chutes. They set their saddles on the horses and pulled at cinches and bucking ropes. Men towered above the ground as they straddled the chutes. They were going to ride, and their preparation was a fine balancing act. The cowboy would first position himself above the animal. He would then gently work his way down the boards and slide his feet into the stirrups. He prayed he could do this all without being shoved into the sides of the chute. He was patient as he took hold of the mark he'd made as to where to hold the rope during his ride. He waited to make sure everything was ready. His weight would send a signal to the horse. And he still had to get set in his saddle—position his spurs high on the animal's shoulders—and then nod for the gate to be opened. All could be for naught if his horse reared and bucked in the chute. I didn't want to be responsible if anyone got hurt. If I watched I could learn, and then maybe I could help.

Joe dismounted and said, "Take Snowball outside and wait for me on the backside of the chutes. I'll need him for the grand entry."

"Yes, sir," and I thought to myself that I had gotten the job.

I took the untied reins and looked up at the almost white horse. Snowball stood sixteen hands and I scratched his withers quickly as I led him out of the arena. Had the horse been pure white, an albino, he could have become blind some day.

I watched the horses run into the numbered chutes. Once the slide gates shut, cowboys began their preparations. Everything had to be ready when the flag left the arena.

"Mount up," Joe's voice was loud enough for everyone to hear. He stepped across the slide gate and touched the apparatus above him to keep his balance. I saw Joe smile as he watched me from his vantage point. I stood directly in front of Snowball's chest. Thirty inches of rein dropped from my left hand and touched the ground. My arm itself was parallel to my body. My right arm bent at the elbow, pointed skyward. My hand, level with my shoulder, held the leather just below Snowball's chin. Joe's horse was quiet, our faces touched. I wondered if Joe saw me lean back for my shoulder to touch Snowball's neck.

When I saw Joe come off the chutes, I separated the reins. I threw the right rein in front of the saddle horn. Snowball's mane and tail were long and brushed soft. He was a show horse. Joe took the left rein, gathered the right, and touched the horn of his saddle. His left foot stepped into his stirrup and his entire body rose. Joe settled into the ornate saddle and found his right stirrup. Backing the horse, he smiled down at me. "I'll bring Snowball back to you for safe keeping."

Joe didn't stay for the national anthem and I took the reins with these instructions; "If you tie Snowball by the steps and stay with him, I'll know where you are if I need him again." Joe must have sensed my disappointment because he said, "Nighttime entries are spectacular, but maybe they've got something in mind for closing out the rodeo today."

Joe worked beneath the voices in the announcer's booth. He took over for his chute boss, calling out the names of animals and the cowboys to ride next. Barrel racers and the fancy trick riders mesmerized the crowd. The events moved smoothly. Joe knew what needed to be done and when, but his chute boss Mike had fun when he did his job.

I handed Snowball's reins to Joe and Bob Mason took over at the chutes. I moved to another spot on the fence where I could see the bulls make their first jump into the arena. The cowboy's gloved hand—held tightly to the rope circling the bull's girth. The ride wouldn't count if he couldn't stay on for eight seconds.

I strained to see the cowboy's position. The sun forced me to squint when the bull exploded from chute number two. Cowboys climbed fences, leaving only the clowns to face the bull. Courageous and dauntless, they stayed with the bull's rider until he was safely out of harm's way.

The bull pounded the earth, twisting his body to rid himself of the man on his back, and the rope around his belly. One, two, three jumps, the bull threw himself off the fence just beyond the chutes. The wood was old. Spikes held the boards to the posts made from telephone poles sunk deep into the hard ground. The poles didn't move, but the boards rocked in the wire bands that helped to hold them in place. The whistle blew. The cowboy was on the ground. The animal was back in the holding pen.

Two thousand pounds of sinew and muscle named Widow Maker was up next. I sat motionless with boards between my legs. The blond Brahma should have been black with that name, but the rider was safe in the dirt. Widow Maker broke two boards away from the telephone

17

poles when he jumped over my section of fence. The weathered boards slid down to rest on my foot.

Horses snorted and men scrambled in their attempt to get away from the bull behind me. I heard the sound of splintering wood and turned to see the bull outside of the holding pen. Men roped the animal, while others grabbed hammers and new planking to replace the broken boards. The planks that rested on my foot were moved back into place. The nails were re-set.

Widow Maker was brought back inside the arena with a half dozen ropes around his neck. Joe's rope circled his saddle horn as he led his bull into the holding pen. The bull was docile now that the bucking strap was gone. Snowball stood quietly beside the bull as Joe reached to the animal's neck and loosened each rope around it. When he finished, Joe grasped all the ropes in one hand, and carefully lifted them over the bull's trimmed horns. He lowered his hand with the ropes in front of the bull's face and released the animal. The gate opened for Joe and then closed behind him. He handed off the ropes to men in the arena. He recoiled and looped his own rope over his saddle horn and nodded for the next bull and rider.

When the rodeo was over, spectators left. Paper cups stood like toy soldiers beneath the wooden seats. A breeze moved in and lifted paper plates and napkins lazily into the air. I approached Joe. "You've been busy," I said with a smile. "And you did a good job, too," I touched Snowball's neck.

Joe grinned when he told me Snowball and the bull, were born the same spring. "Too bad Widow Maker wasn't the last bull of the day. But then, if he was, somebody could have gotten hurt when he was loose in the parking area."

I looked up to Joe and asked if I should feed and water again. He said the animals would appreciate it, but he asked me to get some hot food for us first. Joe pulled a ten from his money clip and said I should buy fry bread and beans. He said we'd eat before I fed the stock and that he had drinks, apples, and cookies at the camper. Joe urged Snowball to a lope and stopped beside one of the clowns. After that, he counted the animals in each holding pen.

I pulled my hat down on my head. The wind was picking up, and I didn't want to lose the hat or the deep-fried bread I'd just bought before I got back to the campground. I found Joe stuffing tents into one side of his horse trailer. He told me to bunk in the camper that

18

night. He thought the rains would come in by midnight and we would likely be the only campers left by morning.

I told him there was no sense in packing wet tents and that my mattress was about gone. Joe nodded and disappeared into the camper. He came out with two round tins. One he placed next to the Coleman thermos. I laid the fry bread on the fold-down table attached to the camper and removed my hat. I poured a mug of water from the thermos and grabbed one of the fry breads. They looked like paper plate tacos and tasted like fresh baked bread. There was a metal bucket of apples nearby.

I asked if his wife sent cookies and Joe pulled in a deep breath and shook his head. He said "Gram bakes" as he put the second tin at the far end of the table. A clown came around the truck and set a third tin on the table. He picked up a paper plate with the deep-fried bread and walked over to our fire ring.

"Jim Bob's the name." The clown reached his gloved hand out to me. I set my mug down and we shook hands. Then he brought his right hand to his mouth and bit one of the fingertips. The glove came off and he repeated the process with his left hand. He left both gloves lay on the ground. He took the folded bread from his plate and began to eat. As I listened to the men talk, they seemed to be old friends. The clown asked about the chute boss named Mike and the others. Before he left, the clown grabbed the tin Joe had left at one end of the table.

I heard him say "molasses," and Joe nodded. The clown opened the tin and took out a cookie. "Just like Mom's," he called back to Joe as he put the whole cookie in his mouth.

I turned to see Joe smile. He looked at his watch and said he had somewhere to go again. He asked me to take care of the stock and bedded Snowball in the trailer before he left. Joe said he would be quiet when he got in and grabbed a handful of cookies. When I looked at the cookies that were left, not a one was molasses.

I found it strange that Joe trusted me. After all, he didn't have any idea who I was. I called my parents from the payphone outside the arena. It was Mother's Day and I had planned to be home by now.

I used a battery lantern so I could see to write. It was quiet—most of the trucks had pulled out just before dark. Jim Bob still had his makeup on when he approached Joe's camp with his camper. He

19

stopped and I walked over to him. I asked why he didn't take off his makeup.

Jim Bob smiled and said nobody would know him if he did. He asked if Joe had hired me. I told him I wasn't sure, but I hoped so. I didn't want to be presumptuous and say something that wasn't true, only to have it get back to Joe.

"He's a good man, and so's my brother Mike." Jim Bob the clown took a deep breath and then coughed so hard I saw tears squeeze between his eyelids. He brought the back of his gloved hand to his face and covered his mouth. I thought he should see a doctor but didn't tell him so. He said I'd like Mike, George, and the others before he drove off.

An hour later I closed my journal and then my eyes. I thought I had this job, but I wondered what would happen when Joe found out I really was a girl.

Chapter 4

I woke to find Joe lying on his bed fully dressed. His eyes were open, and he stared at the ceiling. I'd never heard him come into the camper.

"Did you get any sleep?" I asked as I pushed myself up on my elbows. Joe turned his head—he could have reached out and touched me across the aisle. The look in his eyes told me that he was troubled about something and I wondered if it had *anything* to do with me.

"I know you're a boy. I told the sheriff that's what you were," I thought I heard him mumble. He made no move to sit up and he didn't press me to confirm or deny his opinion of me. Joe sighed deeply. "We've got to get moving once the stock is loaded."

"Does this mean I'm hired?" I asked.

"Yeah, to feed and water. It's an unending task to keep them fat and ready to jump. After I pick up Mike and the others, we'll load."

"Then why don't you sleep. I can feed and water myself."

"If I get them while you feed—that would save time."

"You need to sleep in order to drive. You look exhausted," I told Joe and I said that I'd wake him when I had the stock fed.

Joe rolled over to face the wall of his camper and said, "An hour would help."

I pushed my blanket to the side, shoved my feet into my jeans and then my boots. I stood to zip my pants and left the trailer. When the alfalfa was gone, I peered in the camper window. Joe's chest rose and fell with steady breathing. His body shuddered as I watched, and I

21

thought twice about waking him. The stock needed time to eat and Joe needed his crew to load the animals, so I headed to town, and hoped my initiative wouldn't get me fired. I was sure that the reason he was troubled had *everything* to do with me.

I explained the situation to the sheriff. He agreed sleep was important and he brought Joe's crew from their cells. Texas Tom was a redhead, taller than Joe, and a little heavier. He'd been in fights before, I thought. Hair didn't grow from the scars on his eyebrows. Tom's talk was menacing, but if it came to a fight, I don't think he would take Joe down.

Mike was taller than me, maybe 5'10. I'm sure his life had not been easy; he looked old. Was it years or had it been the kind of life he lived that had aged him? I'm sure Mike spent more time on horses than Tom. His jeans had the imprint of a saddle on them and his boots were well worn. They looked comfortable like my favorite jeans. He was the chute boss and Jim Bob's brother. He didn't move like an old man.

Nathan and John, like Mike, were just shy of six foot. George was a bit taller and the three of them had not said a word. I couldn't make up my mind about them, although I liked Nathan's smile. I thought I saw a sparkle of gold on one of his teeth.

I didn't hear Mike say anything until the Sheriff emptied the contents of plain brown envelopes on the desk. Mike took his wallet and laid down a fifty-dollar bill. He waited for Tom to reach for his wallet and asked, "Do you have it?"

Tom grumbled, but he had the cash. When he had loaded his pockets, he was out the door. Tom cursed when he realized he would have to walk back to the fairgrounds.

The others all came up short. Mike made up the difference, folded his wallet, and slipped it into his back pocket. He curled his hat's brim and positioned it on his head. His hair was dark but speckled with grey. He followed Tom out the door.

George looked at me and John asked, "Where's the boss? Is he okay?" I told them Joe had just run out of time. George nodded and all three silently followed the others outside.

I took a deep breath as I approached the door left open for me. The sheriff didn't say anything about checking on my background. I looked back and thanked him for releasing the men to me. The sheriff smiled and said, "Mike was only doing his job to keep the peace. But you should watch out—that redhead's a *loose* cannon." I nodded and stepped through the doorway as the sheriff reached out to hold the door open. "I'm serious Chris. You may be a tomboy, but you're no match for Tom," the sheriff pushed the door shut behind me.

When I caught up to Joe's crew, Tom looked down at me from his truck cab. "What's next?" His anger had festered to the boiling point as he and the others had walked back to the rodeo grounds.

The battle lines were drawn, I thought to myself and I sucked in a deep breath. "Quit your bellyaching," I told him. I wasn't going to let him take over. "You've loaded this stock before. You know who and what goes where."

I was scared, but I didn't show any fear. "I had to walk both ways to get you out of jail—for your stupid drunken brawl." I turned my back on Tom, and he grabbed for me. I ducked to avoid him. Mike caught his arm just as the others moved in to break up whatever it was that was going to happen next. "Sit on it." Mike spoke three tiny words that were so uniquely his.

"You caused 'nough trouble," George spoke for the first time. "We should've been on de road by ten."

After that, we all worked under Mike's direction, but Tom's anger never totally subsided. I waited until Tom was positioning the last rig before I told Mike I'd go and wake Joe. He looked at me and said, "I think I'll call you Lucky, Ducky," He grinned as John and Nathan brought the loading plank.

I shook my head as I walked away from the three men and then looked back over my shoulder, "The name's Chris," I said.

Joe was startled, first with the light when I opened the door and then by my telling him that the stock was almost loaded. He jumped from his bed and bolted out of the trailer, knocking me to one side as his feet reached the ground. He saw his rigs and broke into a run— stopping at Mike's side. "What the—" Joe turned to me as I approached. "How'd they get out of jail?"

Mike interceded, just as he had earlier. "We paid our fines, and the Sheriff released us." He used Joe's shoulder to push himself into his rig. "You take care of camp and head for home." Mike placed his hat in its holder. "I'll get the stock there." Mike's right hand went to the mic clipped to his dash as he pulled the door to his cab shut. "Nathannnnn-yal, and my Deere John, we're clear to roll for home. Tommy, pull ahead of Georgie and let me get around. I'll lead us in, and boss man will bring up the rear with the youngster we've inherited." Mike glanced over to me and shook his head, snickering loud enough so I could hear. My eyes burned. Mike had called me a child but at least he didn't say I was a girl.

Left alone with Joe, I faced him. Without his hat, he didn't look old, maybe my dad's age. I bit my tongue so I wouldn't say anything that would get me into more trouble. Yesterday, the clown had talked about his brother Mike and I wondered who was related to whom.

Joe had offered me work, but the anger I'd just seen in his eyes frightened me and I thought about leaving—because if I waited too long—I'd have to buy another ticket to get home. Neither of us spoke, as Joe made sure his horse trailer was secure behind the camper. He nodded to his cab and I got in.

Instead of going home I was going in the opposite direction. Out of habit, I opened the glass cover of my watch and with my fingers touched its face to tell the time. Joe stretched in his seat and I glanced over to him. "What's botherin' you?" I asked as I got a drink from the thermos at my feet.

"Yesterday I thought you were a runaway."

"I know—that's what you told the sheriff." I offered Joe water and after drinking it he returned the empty lid. "Why'd you think I'd run away? And what'd you think I'd run from?" I pushed Joe Engelmann for an answer.

He was silent at first and kept his eyes on the road. He finally said, "You were sleeping under the stars and carrying what looked like everything you owned. You didn't have money for food, so I asked the sheriff about you."

"I heard you ask. He didn't have any answers for you, did he?" I took a deep breath and asked, "Is there anything you'd like to know about me?"

"You're not going to make this easy for me, are you?" I thought he was going to leave me along the side of the highway if he didn't get a straight answer from me soon. He spoke again, "I need to know if you are man or woman—girl or boy—male or female. I don't care what you call yourself." He turned to look at me. "Just tell me what you are."

I nodded my head and said—I am a girl, not a boy—a woman, not a man. I am female—if you have a problem with that—tough—because I don't!

Joe had driven for an hour when he slowed his vehicle to a stop at a roadside pullout. He knew he had been wrong—thinking I was a boy. He watched me closely and listened when I talked. I was sure Joe had more questions for me.

He looked at me and said, "You look young, yet you seem mature. I need to check the trailer lights. Will you slide out and let me know if they're all working. I'll do right, left and then brakes."

I dropped to the ground and told him, "I can do anything I put my mind to." As I walked to the back of his trailer, Joe pushed his door open and watched me in his truck's mirrors. I stood behind the horse trailer and nodded as the lights changed.

When he finished, I walked over to the guardrail. Joe followed me to the overlook and said, "I like to stop and walk a bit here."

I leaned over the guardrail to see the ground drop off beside the road. "When I was younger, I was in a car that hit a guard rail in a place like this."

Joe looked at me and asked, "Were you driving? Was anyone hurt?"

"My friend's mother was driving, and she died."

Joe looked at the open expanse before him. I waited for him to say something—anything, and he asked if my friend blamed me for the axe-i-dent?

I trembled when he said *axe*, and I told him we should get back on the road. Joe drove in silence for several miles, and finally, with my eyes closed, I told him I remembered headlights at night and screams that I thought would never end. For weeks after the accident, that was all I could remember.

I reached my hands out to touch the dash of Joe's truck. There was a thick layer of dust from the open windows at the rodeo. "They didn't think I had been hurt at first."

Joe looked at me as if he wanted to hear more, but I wasn't sure just how much I wanted to tell him about a hole in my macula and detaching retinas. "Was there another problem?" he asked quietly.

"After the axe-i-dent," I began, and he looked at me when I copied his enunciation, "No one knew why cataracts began to grow in my eyes. The doctor said they had to reach a certain stage before he would operate. When he did, the surgery didn't work." I paused. "No. I take that back. I was a part of the population that would have problems after the initial surgery. It was just my *luck* to have every *complication*."

"This didn't happen to both your eyes, did it?" Joe glanced over to me.

"It did, but I was afraid to let the doctors operate on the second eye. I put that surgery off as long as I could, but that time when they operated—it worked. I can see with one eye."

"Did you go back to school?" Joe asked.

"I did for a while, but I decided I wanted to travel and see the country."

"You're still in danger of losing your sight?" Joe stared at me.

"It's possible," I said thoughtfully. "But I don't want to think about that."

Joe asked what I wrote about in my journal and his question forced me to think.

He focused on the road ahead and waited patiently until I told him I fill my pages with *thoughts, sights,* and *stories* about the people I've met. I turned to look at Joe's face, "Did you finish college?"

"The ranch came first when my dad got sick and I never went back to finish my studies."

I don't think Joe wanted to talk about himself as he turned the conversation back to me. "You should finish school while you're still young. You'll get a better job than I can offer."

"Why should I, you didn't?"

Joe looked over at me and shook his head. "How long couldn't you see?"

"Long 'nough." I took a cavernous breath.

"How's your friend?" Joe asked. "I think it would be hard to go home to a situation like that." Joe looked at me and then the road ahead of us. I thought he still believed I had run away.

I finally said my friend's father sold their home, but I don't know where they went—I guess I write things down, so I remember what I want to tell Jennifer when I see her. I've looked for her and her father in every town that I've traveled to.

Joe said maybe they'll show up some day when you least expect it. I smiled and nodded, but I didn't think that would ever happen. Joe said it's their loss.

Chapter 5

When we arrived in Horse Springs, Joe tried to leave me with his neighbor. He introduced her to me as Mrs. Montoya, and said, please Gram, keep the girl here—as if he didn't want me in his home. I wondered what I had said or done to alienate him.

The elderly woman placed her hands on her hips and asked— what's your problem?

"I don't want any trouble in the house and I'm afraid there will be if I take her home tonight."

Joe went to the back of his camper and pulled my backpack out. He carried it to the porch and Gram blocked his path. "And you don't think there'll be trouble if the girl stays here." The old woman scolded Joe and I kept quiet.

Joe apologized and asked if we could talk the next day, after he had discussed me with the men who worked for him. I watched him drive around the house, out to the road and into the next drive.

I knew the arrangements for my employment were vague from the beginning, but I had trusted Joe—*I wasn't sure why*—except that the rodeo clown named Jim Bob said he was a good man, *and I believed him.*

"What just happened?" I asked, as a horse ran free in the field. A smoky gray tail and mane waved to me in a gust of wind. "Did he leave me here because I'm a girl? Is that what this is all about?" I moved reluctantly into the house with the old woman. "I told him this afternoon—that I was a girl."

Inside her home, Mrs. Montoya pointed to her couch and poured out a glass of lemonade. She gave it to me before she sat down. "Be glad you did, or you could have found yourself in a room full of men tonight."

"You mean there's only one bedroom in that big house over there?"

Gram laughed and then explained that one end of the house is set up like a dormitory. "That's where most of the ranch hands sleep and that's where Joe would have put you. Everyone has to *learn* how to get along."

I listened to what she said and thought about that morning. I was sure Tom didn't like me, but I wasn't sure about the others. I drank half my lemonade and said, "Maybe I will have to go home."

"You don't want his job?" Gram poured herself a glass and she smiled.

I shook my head, and said, "I mean yes. I want my job."

Gram watched me finish the lemonade, "You'll have to work with Tommy T."

"Did Mike tell you I made them pay their fines and walk back to the rodeo?"

Gram giggled and said quietly, "And all the ragamuffins came home safe and sound."

I watched the old woman nod her head and assumed she had heard five different versions of what had happened that morning. And I was about to tell her, "When Mr. Engelmann hired me—he said room and board came with the job—but he didn't know I was a girl."

Mrs. Montoya took my hand in hers, "Then I'll tell you to go over to the big house and tell Joe that you want a room of your own. Tell him I think that's where you should be."

"But he brought me here," I looked around the woman's home.

"I know what he said, but he can't work with you, if you're here."

"Work with me?" I asked.

"Helping everyone get home to their family is something he believes he has to do. You could say it's his calling." The old woman squeezed my hand, "Joe believes that families need to be together."

"But he's the stock contractor. That's his occupation, isn't it?"

30

"And putting families back together is his mission in life."

"I'm of legal age to live and work where I please." My voice was growing in volume and intensity. "If I have to fight every man over there to keep my job, I'll do it." I was standing by this time, "I'm not a quitter."

"You need to grow up and learn how to get along," Gram said sternly—my stepfather, would have said the same thing. I swallowed the last piece of melting ice from my glass and nodded my head.

"This was good Gram, if I may call you that?"

The old woman answered, "You may."

I thanked her and then told her I would kindly decline Joe's request to stay in her lovely home. "Joe hired me to do a job, and I'll hold him to that job. If you need my help with anything, please call me, otherwise—I want the job he offered me." I hoisted my backpack to my shoulders and adjusted the straps as I went down the stairs. It seemed lighter this evening as I strode resolutely across the field between the two homes.

I was halfway across the field when it dawned on me. I was on my way home when I stopped at the rodeo. I took a deep breath and exhaled. I thought about *Alice and the Looking Glass* when I reached for the front door in the middle of a long porch. I turned the doorknob, opened the door, and tumbled into the rabbit hole.

A huge fireplace was in front of me. On either side were shelves filled with books. The slate floor was polished. There was no carpet, just area rugs. Walls were thick white stucco. Twelve-inch hardwood supports rose from the floor to an open beam ceiling. I set down my backpack when I saw Joe come from behind the fireplace.

"It's big," I said as I looked around the room.

"That's right. What're you doing in here?"

"Don't I need to be in this house—to learn how to get along with the others who work for you? Isn't there an empty room I can use?"

"They're for family," Joe said curtly.

My eyes rested on the fireplace. There were three photographs on the mantle; above it hung an aerial view of the property. "That makes sense. If your family comes to visit, I'll take a couch or go over to Gram's." Joe was silent and I grinned. "You shouldn't have asked that sweet old lady to make room for me when you told me room and board came with my job."

"She sent you, didn't she?"

I shook my head and said, "No! You hired me and said I wouldn't go hungry and I'd have a roof over my head."

Joe explained briefly how his ranch was organized and operated.

"Who cooks?" I asked.

"Everybody—you'll learn if you don't know how. You'll be assigned kitchen duty at least once a week. It's also the day you do your assigned chore in the house."

"Cook and clean. Both the same day—okay. Where do we do laundry? Everything I've got is dirty." I lifted my arm to smell my sleeve.

"Laundry is beyond the kitchen, and it's probably not a bad idea. There is a room to the right of the fireplace that's available near my room. The bunkhouse wing to the left of the kitchen and the other private rooms will be off-limits for you. I'll introduce you to everyone in the morning. Tomorrow I'll have you spend time with Mike. In time you'll work with all the men." Joe looked at me from head to foot, "And most of the horses."

He took me into the kitchen and opened a commercial refrigerator. "We missed dinner but feel free to help yourself to the shelf of left-overs. We go through a lot of water, iced tea, and coffee. Gram's specialty is cookies and lemonade." As Joe pulled out containers, I looked inside and saw two gallons of milk but no beer or soda pop.

"She uses real lemons and puts butter in her cookies. But I like molasses too."

"Mike's the baker in this kitchen." Joe reached into a cupboard and pulled out two metal dinner plates. He handed one to me and removed two sets of silverware from a drawer. He filled his plate, and I filled mine. He slipped them into the oven to heat up.

I was closing containers when Nathan came around the corner. "Is there anything left?" He asked, pausing to look at the wall holding a year's worth of calendar pages with a chalkboard around it.

"Did the others already eat?" Joe asked.

"Yep."

"Then grab a plate, Nate, and join us."

32

I scrutinized the young man. He had a smile on his face when he entered the kitchen that disappeared when Joe called him Nate. Mike was definitely playing with names when he called him Na-thannn-yal at the rodeo grounds. I did not want to make a mistake, so I introduced myself as Chris, short for Christine, and asked, "What do you like to be called?"

"I like Nathan."

"So do I," and asked, "Do we leave the empties in the sink, or should I wash them?"

"I got me the short straw to eat last and clean up." Nathan put the containers with food back into the refrigerator and I quickly rinsed the empties. When our food was hot, we used kitchen towels to carry our plates to the table and protect it. Nathan placed three more plates and cold salads on the counter. Joe filled glasses with water, and we talked over our meal. Now full and relaxed, Nathan's smile was amusing. "I'll get these." He stacked the empty plates and filled one of the glasses with our silverware. His hair was non-existent. He was either bald or shaved his head every day.

"How about I wash, and you put away, so it's done right?" I reached for the faucet and ran the water hot. I rinsed a cloth and called out, "Wipe the table clean." The cloth landed in front of Joe. I hoped that he realized he had not made a mistake in hiring me even if I was a Christine, and not a Christopher. I knew I could and would take charge when necessary. He wasn't going to force me to go anywhere or do anything I didn't want to.

I asked Nathan if he had ridden at the rodeo—he said he lost his draw because of a fight. Joe heard him ask if I'd help him get in some practice and said he'd be there to help.

The rest of the crew was watching television in the next room and Nathan joined them while I showered. Joe had given me a robe to wear so I could wash all my own clothes.

While my clothes were drying, I stood beside a small desk in the front room where Joe was going through the mail. A phone was on the desk, and I asked if I could make a call to my parents. I wanted to give them the address and phone number here at the ranch. Joe said to help myself and handed me an envelope he had just emptied with his name and address on it. His phone number was on the center of the phone base.

After that, I checked out the titles of Joe's books and I recognized several that were in my stepfather's private library. Some things Joe had said today made me think about my stepfather, the man I knew as my dad from the day I was born. He was a doctor—a psychiatrist.

When I was dressed in clean clothes, I went to the kitchen to get a glass of water. I came back to the couch and picked up my journal. Joe looked up and said, "I wouldn't be leaving that outside your room if you want what's inside to stay private."

Public domain is fair game I said, and he smiled. "Point well taken," I conceded. "Who's the giggler?" I nodded to the next room, from where I'd just heard someone stifling a laugh.

He said, "Nate."

"Do you mean Nathan," I asked.

He repeated "Nathan," and I smiled.

Chapter 6

At breakfast Mike said I should come to town with him to pick up work clothes. Those at the table all nodded in agreement. No one approved of my inside out and backwards t-shirt. They all wore long sleeve shirts and jeans in countless shades of blue, brown, and black. Some wore bandanas at their neck, while others had one hanging out of their back pocket. I assumed there was a department store where I'd be able to shop for whatever I might need, but we stopped at a ranch-type general store. Mike looked at me when I left four of the six articles of clothing to be put away by the girl working the front counter.

"You're going to need more than one set of clothes," he said as he laid his hat on the counter.

"Don't worry. I know what fits, so I can pick out others without trying everything on."

"If that's the case, hand them over." He took the shirt and jeans I had chosen, pulled the tags off, and gave the clothes back to me. "Put these on and meet me over at the boots." I told him that I was going to wait on boots, but he shook his head. "Joe said yours were getting thin and he's paying the bill. Pamela, will you pull another eight sets and make one fancy for the Grand Entry?"

Pam took the tags and gave Mike a quick peck on his cheek, "Thanks, Uncle Mike."

When I got to the register, I found her writing up a bill. She asked if I liked the color combinations. I nodded as I put the clothes I'd worn into town on the counter. I asked if Mike was her uncle and Pam shook her head, "Not really," she answered quietly. "He's my mom's uncle. My grandmother and his mom were cousins or something like that. I can't keep the relationships straight."

"So, you're related to the rodeo clown Jim Bob too?"

"Uncle Jimmy." She pointed to the far corner of the building. "Mike's talking to Dad, and half the town's related in some way or another."

Back at the boots, Mike asked if my hat fit and I told him it was a little big. "I'll find you one of your own while Ray helps you try on boots." Mike took off to another corner of the store.

When I had settled on new boots, Mike organized the hats he had stacked in front of him and gave me a black one with a thin leather band. "This one will look good with everything."

The new hat fit better, and I admired myself in the mirror. "Is there anything else I can owe the company store for?"

Mike smiled as he put my worn boots into the boot box and set the hat I'd worn into town on top. "With a light-weight jean jacket you won't embarrass us next week." Mike stopped at boxes of work gloves in various sizes, "Grab a couple pair that fit. You'll need 'em." He looked at my new clothes and pulled a stack of blue bandanas from another bin to add to the pile. Pam looked up and shook her head. He put them back and counted out a dozen red ones. She smiled and kept writing.

Mike thought I should try several horses before settling on the one I would like to do barrels with on the weekends. Our main job between rodeos was to care for the horses, and that included riding all of them. He said that he would set up barrels in the front field, and it would be my responsibility to work all the horses in the pattern. The men didn't like the cloverleaf, and yet Joe wanted to familiarize the horses with everything they might be required to do when sold.

"When you're ready, we'll bring your horse along, so you can ride in the entry and compete. Day money is always good."

As we set up the barrels, I told Mike that Joe was sending in my paperwork. Mike said most of the men would enter the bucking contests; they only needed to take ropes or saddles to the rodeos. He said they all tried to out-rope each other whenever they had free time.

I had watched a half a dozen men walk into the field with ropes that morning. I had seen the dapple-grey with his head held high and tail flying, run in the field. None of the men's ropes had come close to encircling his head.

After lunch, I grabbed an apple, and Mike took me to the field of riding horses. He carried his rope and two halters. "See any you'd like to try? I've seen you look at them since we got home yesterday."

I looked for the dapple-grey. I took a bite of my apple and pointed when I saw him, "That one kept evading everyone this morning."

"Smokey the Bear come over here," Mike called out to the gelding and grinned. I shook my head and thought that he couldn't say a name without playing with it. "He's a hot one. We'll have to teach you how to rope if you want to ride him."

The apple was juicy. I used the back of my hand to wipe the corners of my mouth. "Let me try something. You stay here." I took a few steps, and then looked at my hands, "You better give me a halter." Mike handed me one and stepped into the group of horses to see what I would do next.

I stood still and watched the three-year-old. "You smell my apple, don't you?" I knelt on one knee and said, "If you want a bite, I'll share." There was a stare down. The horse moved, circling, "It's all right Smokey the Bear," I turned to look at Mike and shook my head. "I won't bite." I waited patiently, my hand extended flat and open. "I'm going to take another bite. If you want some apple, you'll have to come pretty soon."

The horse was behind me and he snorted. I felt something wet hit the middle of my back. I lost my balance as Smokey reached over my head and took the apple from my hand. I stood and turned, to slip the halter on him and finger-combed his mane.

Mike pulled one of the unassigned saddles for me and looked at Smokey. He put the saddle back, "If you're doing barrels on Smokey, you better use the Windswept." I remembered the saddle's name from Saturday morning. I touched the leather when Mike returned. He double checked the cinch and judged the stirrup length for me when I was in the saddle. This saddle had the same modifications as the ones the two sisters used.

Mike adjusted the stirrups again and said, "Show me what you know." I took Smokey through five gaits, stopping, backing, and turning him between each one. Once I convinced Mike I could control Smokey, we left the paddock area.

When we got to the front field, an audience waited to watch. Mike walked his horse around the cloverleaf pattern with me several times, and then picked up the pace. Mike dropped out and went to Gram's side while I continued to circle the barrels at a slow trot. Together they watched me ride, pleased that we never once touched a barrel. Mike called me over, "When you feel comfortable, move into a canter, do five rounds with a short break between and then cool your horse down." I wanted to keep riding, but I did as I was told. I knew there would be many hours of practice if I wanted to ride in Oklahoma.

Mike told me that Pam had tried Smokey that spring. After two runs, she had returned the reins to Joe and said, "He's not for me. Smokey was born to run the barrels. He needs someone who'll really go the distance with him. And I still want to design a line of clothing."

That night Gram wore a shawl over her shoulders. She motioned for me to come near and I asked, "Does everyone think I should give up and go home?" I pouted as I climbed the steps to the old woman's porch.

When I reached the last step—Gram placed her hands on my shoulders. She was still holding the ends of her shawl. She looked me in the eye, "You ask this after shopping today and being given the Windswept?"

The next morning, I asked Mike if Gram was his grandma, or Joe's. He smiled and told me, they all lay claim to her, and so could I. I asked how long he'd worked for Joe, and he said he'd known him for a lifetime, but that didn't answer my question.

I studied the calendar board while he restacked and put away the boxes we had used to bring home groceries. There were twenty-four chalk and bulletin board squares that reminded me of a grade school classroom. Joe had penned the rodeo schedule onto paper calendar pages and thumbtacked each month into its own square.

Joe assigned the drivers for each rodeo on a clipboard that hung from a cup hook. There were four chalkboard blocks, all 24 inches tall tagged today, tomorrow, near and distant future. I remembered the discussion over breakfast about the jobs listed in the block tagged today.

At dinner, Joe told Nathan that he should get the bay after we ate. She was docile enough to walk up to in the field, but she'd buck when she felt a man on her back. "Mike, grab a pickup horse; and Chris, we'll get the rest of the gear," ordered Joe.

I got up with my dirty dishes when I heard whispers about Mike roping Smokey for me that morning. I was angry and said, "I'll be outside!" I dropped my dishes into the sink, grabbed an apple from the counter, and abruptly left the kitchen.

I glanced back to see some of the men turn their heads with a look of, 'What just happened?' on their faces.

"Let her go," Mike said. "Let's clean up the kitchen so Nathan can ride at our rodeo. We can put clean dishes away later."

Mike followed everyone out the back door. I was waiting on them and I asked, "So who caught him this time?" I was sitting on Smokey without a saddle. "I've made the decision that this will be my horse to ride when I do barrels at the rodeos. You can keep your ropes off."

Mike grinned from ear to ear as he pulled the door shut behind him. My eyes stopped at Joe, "Do you need to write this down to make it official?"

"No, I'd say this is official enough. Turn him loose, and we'll go help Nathan."

Nathan looked at me as he prepared to let himself down onto the bay. The entire crew was there to watch, and he said, "I'd rather everyone **not** see me get tossed off tonight."

I laughed and told him, "Then don't get tossed. I saw you watching me, and I'm sure we'd both be there to see the others ride." I added quickly, "If Tom and the others weren't such cowards."

"Don't let Tom hear that, or you'll be roadkill."

"I'm not scared of him," I said with a grin.

We hooted and hollered 'til dark that night and then came inside. Morning would come early.

I saw the "Gram" square on the chalkboard at breakfast. No one had said anything about it, and I asked if I needed to pick a day for myself. The days of the week were in the block, and beside each day one or more names were listed, although neither Mike nor Joe's names were in the square. The others burst out laughing, and Joe asked if he needed to restrict my visits. I turned beet red and wanted to crawl under the table and hide. I'd set myself up for that one, but I'd gotten them all the night before. Nobody roped Smokey for me.

Chapter 7

On Thursday, Joe paired me with George, handed me a set of keys, and said to start the blue beast.

"I'm not legal. I don't have my license," I told him.

"You're not going off property, but you'll need a pair of gloves to check the fence line."

George pulled a frozen jug of water from the freezer and then opened the cooler. He'd been quietly making sandwiches and pulling fruit and vegetables from the fridge.

As I stepped on the running board, George checked off what was in the bed of the truck and I heard him say, "Cooler, smooth wahr, bob-wahr, fence boards, posts, and a hole-digger." A tool belt rested on top of a five-gallon bucket. I tossed my gloves on the seat before getting in. George looked past me to Joe's face in the truck window. "You said the 'pointment's at three?" I realized everyone had their own oddities in the way they spoke. Joe nodded as he pushed my door shut.

I thought about asking what the appointment was for, but then I realized the truck was a three in the tree. I looked at the wheel as I put the key into the ignition. No one had asked if I could drive a standard transmission.

George removed his hat. His hair was sun bleached, blond and curly. "You can put your hat inside mine or keep it on your head." He took my hat and positioned both our hats in the hat rack. "Clutch in. Turn the key. Drop it into reverse. Release the clutch as you press

41

the gas. You'll feel the gears engage. Back up. That's good. Clutch in. Bring it up to neutral. Back out of the clutch. Gentle on the gas and glide it into first and den we go 'round the house." George's mispronunciations disappeared when my brain added vowels and dropped consonants.

I looked in my mirrors to see Joe watch me reposition the vehicle to drive it away from the house. He stood with his arms folded across his chest and when Joe turned around, the men who were standing nearby, scattered. I took a deep breath and exhaled, "He could have at least asked if I knew how to drive stick."

"Why?" George asked. "You're driving a stick now." I saw the corner of his mouth turn up ever so slightly when I looked over at him. We followed the drive along the fence to the woods. There was a straight stretch and George had me shift down to second. He instructed my shifting of gears from second to third and back down to second and then first and second— "Brake gently, let the clutch engage, release the brake and accelerate, feel the clutch. They teased me, too, in the beginning. I'm not smart like some of the others."

When I realized I was doing it all on my own, I looked over at George. His face was one big smile, "I'll check the fence as you do the driving."

All morning long I drove. When we found a broken rail, we replaced it. If the board was still good, we re-nailed it to the fence post. Sometimes we'd add wire reinforcing. By eleven, we ran out of boards, and we strung barbed wire between the posts. We placed old boards onto the truck bed. By noon, George handed me the jug of melting ice as he lifted the cooler from the truck. We were under a canopy of trees, somewhere on the ranch. I wasn't sure where I was, but I knew that if I followed the fence line, I'd eventually get back to the main house.

I took a drink from the jug of ice, careful to leave half of the liquid for George as I remembered the day before. Two jugs of thawing ice passed from man to man. We were in the corral after releasing the horses to the field. When the jugs reached me from opposite sides of the circle, there were only chunks of ice. I tipped one jug, and the ice fell toward my face. I waited for droplets of water to reach my throat. Looking at the second jug, I said that I'd add water. As I walked away, they laughed. I filled the jugs from the outside faucet and as they watched, I drank one of the jugs empty. I filled it again, but this time

I slipped my hand into my pocket and removed my father's pocketknife. With my back to the others, I made slits near the openings in both jugs.

When I reached the two men who had given me the ice, I asked if they wanted more water. I told them, "It might not be as cold, but it's still wet." John took a jug and Joe reached out and took the other. I thought I should warn Joe but decided to allow the chips to fall where they would. The men took the jugs and lifted them above their heads. They intended to let water stream into their mouths and down their throats. The slits I had cut allowed the water to dribble from the jugs and that surprised the two men, and the rest of the water poured onto their faces. They choked and coughed.

John yelled, "You little bitch" and dropped his jug to grab for me. Joe coughed and said, "Damn you!" while Paul just stood and laughed. I told them both that if I'd known they wanted showers, I'd have drawn hot water. Mike took the jugs and cut off the necks, allowing the ice to fall to the ground and said they both deserved it today. Paul reached out and gave me a quick hug, and I thought the rest of the crew believed he had been in on the joke.

George had seen it all, and today he told me, "You weren't very nice." I hung my head, not sure how I should respond. "But they weren't nice to you, either."

I raised my eyes to see George smile when he said I had stood up for myself but wasn't mean about what I had done. His sun-darkened skin made his hair even lighter, almost white. We took apples from the cooler and went back to work.

George took the wheel at 2:00. I watched his fingertips make sure the truck was in neutral. He pressed the gas pedal and released the clutch. We moved forward ever so gently. I couldn't feel the shifting of gears, even though I watched his hands and feet. It was as if the truck were gliding on a frozen lake pulled by magnets beneath the surface. I looked to see where I was, but I saw no road, drive, or wheel tracks.

"It's okay. We'll make it by three," George told me.

"We'll make what by three?"

"License Bureau. You can't drive without a license."

I looked at him and asked, "Will you teach me how to drive?"

"You can drive."

"I'm serious George. Will you teach me to drive the way you do? And on top of that, I believe you're smarter than you give yourself credit for."

In town, George turned off the engine. A sign in the window of the sheriff's office indicated driving exams were given after 3:00—it was 2:55. The examination room was just a tiny corner with a vision machine to make sure I could read signs on the road. Even though I was seeing with only one eye, I passed. The written portion was simple, *common sense*—I told myself, but I struggled because I didn't have my glasses with me. I could see well enough without them, unless I needed to read something, and the print was small. *You've done this all before, so do it again.*

George smiled when I came out of the building. An officer waiting with George and he said, "Hop in, Chris. My name's Terry and we'll do the road test now." He was just a hair taller than me and he had dimples, "George says you're ready." His smile was inviting as he stood beside Joe's truck holding the driver's side door open.

I looked at George and shook my head. He grinned from ear to ear. "You're as bad as the others," I told him.

After I had driven, Terry gave me the paperwork I would need for my license and I told George, "I take back what I said earlier. You're worse than the others."

Officer Terry laughed, "You better blame Joe for this one. He said something about paybacks when he called yesterday to schedule this." I realized I better be ready for anything now.

"We'll have ice cream if you promise to eat your dinner," George said when he had me stop at a roadside stand littered with horse droppings. There were ponies tied to hitching posts as children licked at ice cream. I thought about how often my stepfather and I had stopped for the cold treat before dinner. George said, "The twist is on me today."

"Hey, George, who's your friend?" asked a voice from behind a piece of equipment in the tiny building. Eventually I saw a woman come to the counter with two twisted soft serve cones.

"This is Chris." George carefully pulled a dollar bill from his front pocket. He flattened it on the counter and reached for the napkin

44

dispenser to wrap one pointed waffle cone before he handed it to me. The woman took the dollar. "Chris works for Joe now."

"George," the woman sighed. "Didn't I tell you that the next time you brought someone for ice cream, they had to be named Ringo?" I looked mystified, and the woman spoke directly to me, "With George, Paul and John working for Joe, I keep telling them that they've got to find a Ringo. Then I can say the Beatles have eaten here." She placed two quarters in change on the counter.

I laughed and told her, "You can call me Ringo. I'll find a pair of drumsticks to put in my pocket."

"You know about the Beatles?" George asked as I twisted my cone to lick the ice cream.

"Doesn't everybody? I even know who Elvis is."

We finished our ice cream and I drove back to the ranch. We ate dinner and eight of us went straight to bed. At eleven we ate breakfast, and by midnight we were ready to leave for the next rodeo. Someone else had loaded the livestock and food for the weekend. We were only responsible for our personal belongings.

Chapter 8

It was late morning when we reached Durango. I came back to camp after the stock had been unloaded and found the tents had already been put up. I grabbed my bedroll and unrolled it on the ground for a short nap. When I woke up, Joe threw my bedding into the camper and insisted that I would sleep there. I talked until I was blue in the face, but it did me no good.

I rode Friday evening, but I was still fuming about having to sleep in the camper. Joe was the boss, and it was his. I didn't want any special treatment. That would only get me more grief from the men I worked with. They didn't think of themselves as wranglers but cowboys and ranch hands. I wanted to be one of them too.

Joe wasn't in sight when I got back to camp, so I grabbed my things and claimed one of the tents as mine. In the morning Mike told me the boss wasn't happy because I didn't stay in the camper.

I wanted to say the same thing, but I bit my tongue and asked Mike to show me how to rope. He said I should work on my lead change but grabbed his rope and stepped up behind me. His arms circled my shoulders. It felt like it did when Dad taught me to swing a golf club. I could smell Mike's aftershave and I blurted out, how old are you.

"Older than you," he manipulated my fingers and muttered something about me needing to have gloves on. Mike went back to the truck for my gloves and I asked John to get a calf out for me to rope. At Tom's suggestion, he chose the largest calf there was and tied it to a post. I got my rope on the calf and tried to keep it taunt, but the calf pulled out the slipknot John had used. When the calf started to move the rope began to slide through my hands.

Mike saw what was happening, and yelled at me to let go, but I held on tight allowing the rope to burn the skin off my palms. When the rope was gone from my hands—I was on the ground. Mike got to me and told me not to move, but I tried. He threw my gloves to the ground and stopped me. He took my hands in his, winced and said, "That needs peroxide." He yelled at those who were watching, "Has somebody gone for the doctor?"

I told Mike I was okay, but he wouldn't believe me until the doc came and both men helped me to my feet. Doc poked and prodded both my shoulders until he was satisfied that I had not dislocated anything. He slipped a cloth sling around my arm saying he wanted to give my shoulder a rest. He said I'd be able to drive when the time came to go home.

I heard Joe's voice from the open door of the first-aid trailer asking what happened. He'd heard me cry out. Mike looked up just as the doctor poured peroxide over my hands.

I tried hard not to cry when Doc put some salve on my palms and told me to keep them clean. He wrapped gauze over the salve and taped it down. "No more dirty work or roping until the rope burn heals."

I said, yes sir, as I turned to look at Joe. "I roped my first calf," I told him proudly and then bulldozed my way between the men.

"Did she tell you she's had cataract surgery and complications from it?"

"That doesn't have a thing to do with today," I yelled at Joe and the others.

Mike asked me later if I was blind.

I shook my head and told him, "I can see with one eye, but I am legally blind in the other. And some day, I could lose the sight I have."

I don't think Mike wanted to hear that.

On Saturday evening I rode Smokey into our camping area. As I approached, I saw Joe take my sleeping bag from the tent and place it in the camper. Mike asked him what he was doing, and Joe answered, "Chris is staying in the camper, and at home she's moving to Gram's." Joe tossed his sleeping bag into my tent.

I waited to hear what Joe would say next, but Mike said I was as bad as the rest. I thought to myself, I was becoming friends with the men I worked with, and I was proud that they thought of me as one of the guys.

Joe told Mike that I had gotten hurt today. He said that I lived and traveled with men and he was sure people would think I wasn't a "good girl." I heard him say, "If she moves over to Gram's, she can stay home—problem solved."

Mike shook his head when he saw me. "She won't stay home. Rodeo has a death-grip on her like the rest of us." He raised his hand and with an exaggerated motion waved his arm to take in all those around the arena.

I held onto my saddle and removed my right foot from its stirrup. Standing in the left stirrup, I brought my right leg over Smokey. I leaned forward on the saddle seat to balance myself and kicked my left foot loose, so I could slide off. I didn't see Mike behind me, and he grabbed hold of my belt and didn't let go of me until my feet were on solid ground. He broke at least two belt loops. "Whoa little lady. Stop right there. This is just the reason doc harnessed that shoulder." He released my cinch and lifted my saddle—watching me the entire time. I told him I was sorry, and he carefully put his arm around my shoulder and walked me to our fire ring. "You," he said turning to face me, "Have turned life at the ranch upside down in one very short week." I bit my lower lip so I wouldn't make him mad by smiling.

Joe was at the fire, and he didn't look happy. The others had already gone off somewhere, and Joe left without saying a word to me. That night I asked Mike about everyone who worked for Joe. When I asked about the boss—Mike said he was married once and so were some of the others. Several had girlfriends, but nobody had a steady, except for him. He said, "Grace and I go back a long way."

I looked at Mike when he said Joe still believes he's married. "Good God it's been more'n twenty years since his divorce." Then he got quiet and put another log on the fire. "I think you're just what we needed this summer. The times, they are a changin' for all of us." Mike looked at me and asked, how old I was.

I grinned and said, "Younger than you," mimicking his earlier response. He smiled and accepted my answer, but I went on to say— I'm of legal age to live where I please—get married without asking anyone's permission—or go to war and fight in the jungles of Vietnam if they'd allow girls.

After that, Mike said it was late and that I should sleep in the camper, no musical bedrolls.

I saw Jim Bob inside Doc's trailer when I returned my shoulder harness, but we didn't have a chance to talk.

On the drive home, I asked Joe if he had any children. I told him Mike said he was married a long time ago. He didn't want to hear what I had to say, so at our first break I asked George if I could ride with him. Joe seemed relieved by my decision.

I learned a lot about George that night. His father had homeschooled him, and he had learned math skills by calculating distances and geography from travels with his father. He told me about all the constellations when it got dark. He was taking classes by mail but never said he wanted to do anything but work for Joe.

When we arrived home, Joe took my things from the camper and told me to come with him. We walked across the field to Gram's and he set my things against her home. She hurried to the door in her nightgown while we waited on the porch.

"Come inside," she said when she opened her door, but like the week before, Joe didn't move.

"You keep the girl here. She can work the horses, but she stays out of my house." His commands were short and to the point. Joe never called me by name.

Then it was my turn, "Who's going to hurt me? You have decent people working for you. They might give me a hard time, but I can dish it out, too. If you send me away, somebody's going to wonder why." I stepped right up to Joe and got into his face, "And then they'll really start asking questions." There was a fire in my eyes, and it came out of my mouth. "If that happened, I could add fuel to the fire. I could cause you a lot of trouble." Joe stepped away from me and I saw fear in his eyes.

I never looked at Gram. My mother would have slapped me right across my face. I grabbed Joe's shirtsleeve and tried to redeem myself. I was playing a hunch when I told Joe his wife was younger than me when he married.

I snatched my backpack and headed back across the field. This morning, Joe followed me into his home. He leaned on the back of the chair where I had set my things.

"Your parents don't know me, and I was married at your age, and she was young—we both were. Now—I don't have a wife or even a daughter here in the house." We faced off with the chair between us. "Some of the men who work for me don't want you here."

"I know that. So do my parents. I told them last week when I sent my finished journal home. If they've got a problem, they've had the time to write, or they'll tell me when I call later." I walked over to the telephone, "Maybe there's a letter here."

I put my glasses on and thumbed through the unopened mail. One postmarked Oklahoma was for me. "If you want to know what they have to say, read my letter." I tried to hand the envelope to Joe, but he turned away, leaving me alone to read my mail. I slit the envelope and withdrew two sheets of paper. I sat on the couch to read, first in my stepfather's hand.

Chris,

It was wonderful to receive your letter written on 10 May last week, although we'd expected you home. Just knowing we can reach you if there's an emergency gives me peace of mind.

The people you describe in your letter, Joe Engelmann, Mike, and Mrs. Montoya, seem to be good and kind people. Concerning the others, I feel many of them may wish for some misfortune to befall you. Although I believe you and others are well aware of their intentions.

I assume you are working hard at befriending these men, but please be careful. I know you can dish things out as well as the next. I WILL trust your judgment in knowing how much pushing to do.

Your mother is voicing her own thoughts. I wouldn't attempt to speak for her tonight.

Forever and a day,

All my love - Dad

51

I whispered a prayer of thanks, and then I heard Joe's voice, and his boots come across the floor.

"When do you leave for home, or are they coming to get you?" he asked sitting down to wait.

"You're wrong," I handed my dad's letter to Joe and he read each word carefully, so that there would be no misinterpretation. I think my dad knew his letter was not for me.

Joe's eyes moved to the letter I still held in my hand. "My Dearest Christine," Joe mused, as he looked at my mother's letter.

I stood up and faced Joe, "I told you before, my name's Chris! I haven't read this one." I held the piece of paper between us.

"But you knew what they would say when you wrote to them. You offered me the envelope unopened." Joe went on to speak in a hushed voice, "Your mother's handwriting is beautiful, so similar to my wife's."

I looked at the letter still in my hand and I sat back down. Joe read from beside me—

My Dearest Christine—

In your journal, I have seen you grow and mature these past months. Your words have comforted and calmed me in the night when I couldn't sleep.

I was distraught and fearful when you wrote about sleeping in bus stations and spending nights outside on the streets.

Now I believe you needed to make this journey on your own—to become the woman you were meant to be. Gregg was right. I had to let you go and I am glad "Gram" is there for you. I can only express my regret that your own grandparents died so long ago. Treasure this woman and trust her judgment. When you deal with people, use kindness as your weapon, it's a mighty big stick and employs a power nothing else can equal.

I wish that I could be nearby my love—

Mother

Chapter 9

At six-thirty, the rodeo crew staggered to the breakfast table with hair uncombed. We poured bowls of *Wheaties* to eat while we caught up on the local news. After that, most went back to bed.

I was still at the table when Tom returned to the kitchen. I watched quietly as he went to the freezer and removed one package of frozen meat. In the refrigerator's crisper section, he shuffled the fresh vegetables. He brought ten pounds of potatoes from the pantry. I looked at the chalkboard to learn Tom was to work alone that day. He pulled the grocery list and when he turned to the table, he hesitated, realizing I had not gone to my room.

I watched him write 20# potatoes, 15# carrots, bag of Vidalia onions, 5 roasts, milk, and eggs. "Dinner sounds good," I said. "Want some help peeling potatoes or carrots?"

"No." Tom was blunt; he folded his list and slipped it into his shirt pocket. "I scrub them with a brush. Go back to bed." He reached for a set of keys on his way out the door. The empty grocery boxes were already outside, and Joe paid all the bills.

I leaned forward and slept for twenty minutes. Refreshed from the power nap, I thought now is my chance to explore the room everyone shares without anyone bothering me. There were televisions at both ends and an upright piano. I spun a full circle before I turned back to the Baldwin. Against it leaned three guitar cases. I smiled, thinking that several men must play. A violin case was on top of the piano. I thought back over the meals I'd eaten and tried to remember the men's hands. There were no piano hands as my teacher would call them, long and slender fingers having the agility to reach octaves and full chords.

I lifted the piano key cover—I walked my fingers up the 88 keys, a half step at a time—they all responded. I pulled the bench out, sat down and remembered the chromatic scale—chords next, my teacher had made me do them every time I practiced.

I closed my eyes and I could still hear my teacher say, "Now we have Christine, playing Beethoven's *Fur Elise* written for the love of his life." My fingers were cold when I came to the Steinway. I slipped my hands between my thighs and the bench, warmed by my best friend and teacher's daughter. I never liked to go first. The bench was always cold.

I saw pages of notes spread out in front of me. Music filled the house as my hands moved in synchronization up and down the keyboard. My fingers touched the keys, black and white, sharps and flats. I had played the piece so often, the muscle memory remained. I felt chills up and down my arms. I couldn't believe that I'd remembered every note I'd practiced for months before the accident that killed my teacher. I brought my hands back to the keyboard and played again, confidently for Jen's mother and my teacher. When I finished the second time, I reached out to cover the keys. *Maybe I would see my friend again.*

Only then, did I see that Mike had been watching. "I'm sorry that I woke you," I told him.

Mike smiled as he shook his head, "It hasn't been played like that since Joe's mom gave lessons."

"I shouldn't have assumed."

"It's there to be played—only no one knows how." Mike asked if I knew other pieces. I told him I'd need music after all this time. He said he'd look for some and ask Joe if he had put them away for safe keeping.

I was fully awake, so I went to the pantry and found the bucket of dusting supplies. I began at the doorway and dusted all the furniture. I picked up everything that I came across. When I reached the piano, I dusted the foot pedals that I'm sure everyone forgot. The bench was heavy—so I opened it and found a whole stack of sheet music, songs from the 20s and 30s, but nothing from recent years. Maybe I could find something in town if there was a music store. The Beatles or Simon and Garfunkel were my favorites.

I had just put the cleaning bucket away when Tom returned with the groceries. I told him what I had done and didn't wait for a reply. *Kill him with kindness*—I smiled as I went back to my room.

After lunch was over, Tom layered meat, onions, carrots, and potatoes into the roasters and turned them on. He was ready to do his inside chores without interruption. When I went to leave the house, I could hear the sweeper in the next room. I grabbed an apple for Smokey but came back to the sink. I quartered and cored the apple and halved the quarters again. I opened one of the two roasters on the counter and tucked the eight bits of apple into the potatoes. Tom had used red-skinned potatoes, so I thought the apple would go undiscovered if he opened the lid.

Just before dinner, Tom separated the vegetables, sliced two of the roasts onto platters and made gravy from the first roaster. The platters made it around the table once before they were empty, and I had only taken a small portion. Tom filled the serving platters again and made more gravy before he sat down and served himself. I took a second and larger helping and savored the flavors on my tongue.

Tom tasted his meat, and with his fork, found a piece of apple skin. He looked over to me and said I could add it to both roasters the next time.

Mike asked "What?" as he looked between us.

Tom moved the food around on his plate. "It's a family secret, leave it at that."

Chapter 10

I was prepared to ride in Cuervo on Friday evening when Mike brought my number to me. "There's no mistake today," Mike said as he pinned a sheet of heavy paper to Smokey's blanket. Then he laughed as he pulled my foot from the stirrup.

"What did I do now?"

Mike looked up, "Nuthin, but I'm glad you got your hair fixed. We were tired of looking at you twice to remember you're a girl. Now go for it, pretty lady."

Jim Bob gave me two thumbs up when I entered the arena. When I completed my race around the barrels, I asked Joe how my time compared to the others. He said the best so far was Tina Mason at seventeen-twenty and I remembered Tina's husband from Santa Rosa.

"She's pretty high up in the standings," Joe said as he dismounted. "I'll ask Tina to give you pointers on the lead change and how to do your cool down circle more effectively."

"Would she help me?" I asked, "We compete against each other."

Joe smiled, "All I have to do is ask."

"Is she at every rodeo?" I pouted. I liked being the center of attention and I was the only girl at the ranch, but on the weekend— there were other women. Joe and Mike knew them all. After dinner, Joe introduced me to the Masons properly, and I learned that Joe was Tina's godfather. He had agreed to be the man of the hour when he was only ten years old. In my head, I tried to calculate everyone's ages and I realized there was no reason for my jealousy. Tina was married and Joe was too old for us both—*I still had some growing up to do*—I thought to myself.

Tina said we would work together in the morning.

By eight the next night I was exhausted, but Mike said I'd look as "purty" as a picture if I wanted to go to the dance in my contest clothes. I looked at the crew. It would have been okay if I tagged along, but they'd have to wait for me to shower again. I stretched my arms over my head and yawned, "Not tonight. Go without me."

Joe wanted to stay back, but I whined, "I don't wanna to go, so leave me alone. I've got good company with the horses." Then I smiled, "Be good boys and behave yourselves, I don't wanna be stuck without any help tomorrow." They all laughed, and the sound of their voices trailed off as they went down to the dance.

For months I had traveled alone. Now I rarely had a minute to myself. A thin band of light identified the building housing the showers. I grabbed an old t-shirt and a pair of shorts. Removing my boots, I put on a pair of flip-flops—at least that was what Mike called them. They slapped the bottom of my foot every time I took a step. I looked at the clothes I held in my hand, knowing Mike wouldn't approve. He never wore anything other than boots, jeans, and shirt with a tie around his neck. Joe dressed the same. Smokey snorted as I moved beside him. "Keep an eye on camp for me."

I followed the path to the showers where a single bulb illuminated the room. Curtains in front of the privacy stalls cast shadows. I tossed my clothes and towels over the curtain rod and placed my bottle of shampoo on the floor. I heard something and stepped outside to circle the building. With the music from the dance, I couldn't tell where the sounds were coming from or what they were.

I heard someone say hello and turned to the voice. "I didn't mean to startle you," a man remarked, stepping into view. "Would you have a towel I can use? Somebody swiped mine." He came toward me. "We could walk down to the dance later."

I shook my head and said, "I'm not going down, but I do have an extra." I disappeared into the shower room and returned with a towel. "Just hang it on the post when you're done, I'll get it later."

"Yes ma'am," the man vanished around the corner. Back inside, I heard water running. Tonight, the water was hot, and I added some cold, thinking that cool showers really weren't that bad. Especially on hot and sticky days like today.

I dried my body and wrapped my wet hair as I dressed. At the entrance, I grabbed the towel I had loaned the stranger. I hung them both to dry by the trailer before I turned to the horses, "I'm not sleepy now." I rubbed Smokey's muzzle, and thought I'd straighten camp for the morning.

Just then, the man from the showers appeared in front of me. I stepped to one side, but he moved, deliberately blocking my path. "Do I scare you?" he asked.

"You surprised me. I have things to do before the others get back." I straightened my shoulders—determined not to show the fear that was quickly taking control of my body.

The stranger stepped closer, saying, "They won't be back any time soon. It's only ten."

I searched for an escape—the horses snorted—something wasn't right. The stranger reached out for me. I was no longer startled. I was terrified when I screamed, "Get out of here! Leave me alone!"

The man grabbed me—his face just inches from mine. "I want what they're gettin' from you."

I tripped out of my flip-flops. "We take care of the stock. That's all we do," I cried out as he pushed me to the ground. He opened his pants, exposing himself and I closed my eyes. I tried to turn away, but my head was held tightly between his legs. I gaged when my throat filled with something thick. I lay paralyzed in fear until the man pulled me off the ground. He lifted my t-shirt and twisted it around my arms. He forced me against a tree, and I fought him blindly with all the strength I had. His abrasive sandpaper-hands pulled at my clothes and I felt his claw-like fingers inside me, "No—oh God—no!" When my skin was raw and sore, I felt him inside of me. He released another erection and I screamed—but I couldn't hear my cries. When he pulled out—he sucked each finger clean, "Oh, so sweet. I'd marry you, to get this every day." He tried to push his face between my legs.

"They'll come after you!" I squawked. And he said, who's going to believe a slut like you? I felt the stubble on his face and his tongue—inside me. The horses reared up. They had been fighting the tether line this whole time. I opened my eyes and heard the horses piercing squeals that should have awakened the dead. I screamed as the stranger moved away and looked for men with weapons, but there were none—just the hooves of a white stallion and a smoky grey gelding that came down on him. He scrambled to his right—and then he was gone.

I couldn't see through my tears. I untangled my shirt from my arms and covered myself. I pulled my shorts back on and went to the horses—I slipped under the tether line and touched each animal's neck. I felt them sidestep, and there we stood—the three of us, breathing heavily. Had the man screamed? Had hooves come down on him or was it my imagination?

In time, I grabbed the work shirt and jeans I had worn that day. With my arms full, I hurried back to the showers. I gagged myself with the handle of my toothbrush and flushed the toilet. I peeled off my t-shirt and shorts, dropping them to the floor of the shower. The hot water scalded my skin. When the water turned cold—I reached for a cloth and my soap. I scrubbed myself everywhere he had touched me and washed my mouth out with soap. My skin was on fire and it burned. I was standing in water and I kicked my clothes off the drain where they had landed.

When I turned the water off, I brushed my teeth. I reached for the clothes I had worn that day and I struggled to get them onto my wet body. I ran barefoot back to camp and I saw Joe's flannel shirt from that morning and slipped it over my own. Inside the camper I bolted the door shut. Water wicked its way from my scalp and dropped to my back and shoulders. I lay down and covered myself. I wanted someone to hold and comfort me and I knew Jen would never judge me.

When Joe's crew returned after midnight, I cautiously left the trailer for the fire circle. I felt safe in the fact that Joe and the others would protect me. I added kindling, limb wood and two logs to the coals before flames burst in front of me.

Joe stirred when the fire blazed. Knock it down, he yelled. It's too big.

Mike came from the opposite direction, "You're too close." They pulled me away from the flames, but I fought them. George and John, both in their boots, kicked at the burning logs, and rolled them in the dirt.

With the fire under control, George reached out and touched my face, "What happened? Your hair's all wet."

I turned away and said I had a hot shower.

Mike reached for my arm and I recoiled. He looked at Joe's shirt over my own, and it too was wet. "You showered with clothes on?" Mike exchanged glances with Joe. "John, get a wool blanket or maybe two." John returned to drape a blanket over my shoulders. He passed a second to George to tuck around my feet. I kicked at him and he went to stand by the others.

"We shouldn't have left her alone," George told them.

From behind me, John asked what was wrong and *I couldn't tell him how stupid I felt.* John went to Joe's side. He wanted him to ask if I'd been raped.

When Joe didn't say anything, John moved to Mike and said that if I had been raped—they had to do something to help me.

Mike watched me and he asked John, "Why do you think you know what happened?"

"Because my sister killed herself," John said. "After someone raped her."

Mike filled his lungs with hot summer air, and expelled it before he said, "Chris might talk to another woman."

Joe went to find Tina and Bob came back with them. I was shaking when Tina got to my side and said a man had tried to grab her near the showers.

The police came and gathered evidence—my shorts and my shirt at the showers. They saw blood and they photographed the horses' hooves. They took us to the police station and questioned me about what I'd said, and what I'd done, and where my underwear was. Worst of all, they took photos. At the hospital, a nurse told me to come back next week and they'd check to see if I was pregnant. I never wanted to see any of them again.

My brain told me I should talk to someone, but I couldn't talk to the people in that town. They didn't know how to help me. And I don't think they wanted to.

I needed my friend and I decided that when I was alone, I'd write down what happened in my journal. But I didn't know how much I would write—or if I would just say I had been raped. I wished Smokey had hit him in the head when he reared up. I truly wished the rapist was dead and I made myself stop crying.

Chapter 11

Caught in traffic, we would have missed the Grand Entry had our clothes not been laid out and our horses saddled. Mike played none of his name games that afternoon, and I could feel that everyone was watching me.

At the end of the performance, the stock was loaded out quickly. Joe sent George and John back to the campground with the horses and I went with them.

George closed the tailgate of the horse trailer. "People shouldn't hurt people," he said, and then he kicked the trailer tires.

When George had gone, John asked if I would be all right. I sucked in a deep breath and he said, "It happened right here. Didn't it?"

I turned to look at him, "Did the cops tell you it was my fault too?"

John shook his head. "You're going through the same hell I think my sister did, but you don't have to do this alone." John touched my hand, "My sister killed herself when this happened to her."

I said I'm sorry, and I attempted to wipe tears from his face, "Are you gonna to tell the others about her?"

"It's about time I told someone." And with that, I knew I would have a full regiment of bodyguards watch me for as long as I worked for Joe.

When we were miles away from the town of Cuervo, Joe asked what I would tell my parents.

I said, "I don't know how to tell them what happened," and I looked out of the truck window. I began to chew on my knuckles.

"Your parents may want you to come home, so they can take care of you," Joe said quietly.

"I don't want to think about that." *By going home, it would mean that I hadn't grown up.*

"Do you want me to call your family? I could explain what happened. It was our fault."

"No!" *I needed my friend,* and I looked at Joe, "I don't want anyone to know what he did to me. I've got to handle my dad just the right way."

"Handle?" Joe quizzed me on the words I had used.

"What did I tell you about my dad?"

"You never told me much about your parents."

I nodded and said Dad's a mind doctor, a psychiatrist. He helps people get through things like this. But if I ask him to come, or go home, Mom would be sure to find out, she's a teacher. "I need to do the right thing for both of them."

"You have to do the right thing for yourself," Joe told me. "Your father would know how to help both you and your mother."

"He's not my father!" I screamed at Joe and I filled my lungs with air. "My father died in Korea, before I was born. He never knew about me." I turned to look at Joe and he appeared to have gone somewhere far, far away.

I think Joe had questions—and I know—I had questions. I think those unanswered questions haunted us both that day. Joe finally told me I was right, "Your dad shouldn't have to help you through something like this, no Father should."

I closed my eyes as miles registered on the odometer—everyone was engrossed in private thoughts—about me, my rape and what, if anything, they could have done to keep it from happening. Had they stayed in camp I'd have been safe, but would another girl have been attacked?

"It hurts me to see you in this much pain." Joe reached out to touch my shoulder.

I nodded my head and went back to looking out the window. I took a deep breath. "He said I asked for this. He said nobody would believe me," and I hesitated, "a slut like me."

"You're nothing of the kind. I don't want you to believe anything he told you—you didn't ask to be raped; no woman does."

Three hours out from the ranch, Joe called "bean time" and pulled his vehicle off the highway into a restaurant parking lot. The others followed. When we entered the restaurant, Joe and his men encircled me. A table of young men laughed at a joke, and Mike glared at them. Joe's crew was impressive, tall and muscular. You wouldn't want to fight one, much less the entire group. We rearranged tables to sit together. A server appeared, and Joe shook his head as she attempted to pass out menus. He stood at the head of the table and said, "Seven specials and coffee all around." When the server was gone, Joe said, "I don't want you in my house tonight." I looked up—Joe was in pain, as was every one of us at the table. "I'd like to call Gram now, so she can expect you."

"You can come back to the house tomorrow, but not tonight." Mike said as he touched my hand.

When Joe returned to eat his meal, he said he told Gram that I needed to sleep. He said she'd put brandy in my lemonade. Each man poured a second cup of coffee. On our way out the door, Joe laid two twenties at the register, and at two Gram took me into her home and closed her door on the men I worked with.

We sat on Gram's couch for a long time and drank tall glasses of lemonade until she was so sleepy, she couldn't keep her eyes open. I covered her with a blanket and quietly slipped out of her home.

The lights were still on in Joe's house and when I approached the front porch, I could hear everyone who had been in Cuervo with me. I didn't want to interrupt them, so I sat down next to the screen door to listen. I heard John say I should see a doctor.

Joe asked what he would do if I wouldn't agree.

"We'll help Chris get better," George said quietly but with conviction in his voice.

I heard footsteps and voices fade away as men left the room. I moved so I could look inside, and I saw Joe face Mike and say today is long from being over.

Mike asked if Joe was thinking about the boy and he nodded. I wondered who they were talking about until Joe said Terry has courageously moved past the abuse and violence. And with our help,

Chris will be able to do the same., Mike said as they walked out of the room.

No one thought to close the front door and I went inside. I heard some of the men discussing what they thought had happened in Cuervo.

Let the boys be boys. We all know what they want by the way they dress—You know you're wrong—What makes you the expert. You know they want it. They're asking for it.—Awe, com'on let the boys be boys. How should we know what they want—You know they want it—They're asking for it. "'Nough," George shouted, stopping their individual voices in my head. "Listen to John. I think he knows what happened to Chris and how we should help her."

I turned away when John began to talk about his sister. I went to my room where I wouldn't hear their voices. I lay down but I couldn't stop their voices in my head.

Across the hall, the door to Joe's study was open. I thought I heard a desk drawer open and then get slammed shut. I heard the telephone being dialed and I wondered who Joe was calling in the middle of the night.

"Doctor, will you take my call in private." Joe gave out our number at the ranch to someone and said he'd expect a call back in 20 minutes. When the call came through, there didn't appear to be any introductions when Joe said, "Chris has been raped." He tried to explain what had happened at the rodeo grounds, the police station, and at the hospital. He said I can only imagine the verbal abuse and the trauma the rapist inflicted on Chris's mind and body.

I was humiliated by the talk in the kitchen and now I listened to Joe discussing me with someone I didn't know. "Good God Gregg,"—I sat up when I heard my stepfather's name. "How can Chris ever get over something like this? How can any of us?"

I went to my door just in time to see Mike go into Joe's study. "Grace is talking to the men in the kitchen. She'll stay over and talk to Chris in the morning."

We should wait and see about that, Joe said. "Her dad's a psychiatrist, and he might want us to go a certain direction in getting her help. I'm talking to him now."

"Do you mean to send her home as punishment, for being a bad child?" Mike seemed angry as I watched his leg move to and fro from the corner of Joe's desk.

I shook my head as I walked across the hall and went into the room. I stood in front of Joe's desk and I looked at them both—first one and then the other. I said, "Don't send me away. This is my home and I don't want to leave." I was crying, but my voice was loud and strong enough that I was sure Dad heard me on the other end of the phone line. "Stop talking about me," I cried, and I went back to my room.

I leaned against my doorframe and listened to Joe tell my stepfather, "Gregg, it's more than your girl—it's every man who works for me—and both of us! We have to work hard to ensure that everyone comes out of this whole. We have people here who can help Chris navigate through this. But we'll need to help each other so we're tough enough when she asks for our help."

It sounded as if Joe was crying when he asked how does a woman ever get over something like this? The act of a man and woman coming together to create a new life is so natural—will any of us ever be able to get past the pain we know she's experienced?

I was exhausted when I lay down on my bed and finally—I slept. In the morning I woke to find Mike sitting in my doorway. He smiled as he pushed himself up the door jamb. "I just wanted to be nearby if you had a nightmare."

I sat up in my bed and asked if I did.

Mike smiled and came to stand at my side. "No—but you snore. Get a shower and I'll fry up some bacon and eggs." He was gone and my door was shut before I pushed back my covers.

A woman was talking to Mike when I came into the kitchen. Those who had been in Cuervo had gone to bed. Others went outside to work. The woman introduced herself to me and said her name was Grace. She said that if I wanted to talk to a woman, she'd listen. I tried to smile when Mike kissed her on the cheek—*I didn't want to talk to a stranger.*

Joe joined us after Grace left and officer Terry arrived and placed a folder on the table. As I watched him—I wondered how long it had taken for him to get over whatever it was that had happened to him.

Joe sat beside me, and Mike cleared the dishes. Terry slid a photo across the table. I started to shake and pushed myself away when Terry said the man who had raped me wasn't in jail. Mike restrained Joe, until Terry said the rapist had fallen onto the road near the rodeo and died. It's my fault he's dead I said.

Terry rejected any thought of the rape or the man's death being my fault. He said metal shoes on hooves do a lot of damage. I'm surprised he made it ten feet, much less a hundred yards to the road.

Mike wanted to know who the rapist was. Joe asked if there were other victims. Terry said he'd find out, but that this was over for me. There would be no court, no trial—no publicity. I asked for the photographs they had taken.

Officer Terry was young, and I wondered if what had happened to me—would make me wise or destroy me. I wished this officer—or one like him—had been there that night. It wasn't so much what he said, but his eyes—they were kind and reassuring. Terry wanted me to talk with Dr. Grace, but I said no. I would talk to my dad—he was a psychiatrist, a doctor.

When Officer Terry left, he said I could talk to him later—if I changed my mind. Mike nodded his head and I just looked at him for a long time. I jumped when the phone rang and Mike placed his hand on my arm, "Calm yourself, I've got this." I moved away and looked back when he asked if he could talk to my dad.

I went to the living room and picked up another receiver. I listened to Mike say someone would always be watching. And that they'd help me through this.

When I was alone on the phone with Dad, I specifically told him not to ask me anything. I think he understood why I didn't want to talk to him.

I called home and told my mother I had kept a friend from being raped. She said she was glad that I had a new friend—and she said that I was a strong woman, but I think she knew the truth—that I needed my best friend. After that I cried myself to sleep on the couch. When I woke up—Joe reminded me that there are people who will listen, when I'm ready to talk.

Officer Terry brought the photographs and I started a fire. When flames filled the fireplace, I threw the envelope into them. The edges curled. They smoked and burned. I watched until the logs were nothing but ashes, then I took the poker and made sure there was nothing left—of the rape, of the envelope, or the contents.

Because he's dead, and horses don't talk, I thought—no one will ever know I had tried to be kind—before he raped me. Alone in my room, I took a razor blade—I removed several tear stained pages from my journal, and I placed the razor blade in my desk drawer. It was too sharp to throw away and could be used again.

I slipped the pages beneath my mattress—thinking that some day I would burn them.

Chapter 12

On Thursday, I had a good day. I rode every horse Joe had in training. I worked each one with whatever saddle they had on their back. I hoped that I would win a buckle over the weekend.

I was dizzy by lunch and exhausted by five, but there was no smell of dinner being ready to eat when we came into the house. Our lunch dishes were stacked at the sink just as we had left them.

It was George's day to cook, but nobody knew where he was. No one had seen him since lunch. Then I saw his note on the board—

Joe will pick up pizza for dinner —

I have to take care of something —

I'll see you all at the rodeo — George

There was no mention of what the something was, or where George had gone. If anyone else knew what was going on, they didn't say, but at five Joe showed up with pizza, cold beer, and soda pop.

I couldn't sleep very well that night, wondering what required George's attention away from the ranch. I didn't want to think it could have anything to do with me. I was almost in a deep sleep when I heard voices outside my room. "George said that he asked for you." I didn't hear anyone answer, so I got up and went to my door. The door across the hall from mine stood open and Mike sat on the corner of Joe's desk again. "You need to go," Joe said. "George said not to waste any time in getting there."

Mike shook his head, "I can't do that." I heard Joe say again, that Mike needed to go. "FINE!" I watched Mike stand up. "I'll go! But I hope to God, this will put an end to it."

When he had gone, I stepped into the hall and asked Joe what was wrong. He hesitated at first, and then said, "It's Mike's brother. I'm going to take Mike to him, but I'll be back in time to get the stock to the rodeo."

I watched from the living room as Joe's pickup moved down the driveway. I wondered why had George and not Mike gone to Jim Bob? I remembered how bad the clown's cough sounded two weeks before. Tonight—I felt as if I'd intruded on something very personal and something Joe didn't want to discuss with me.

I went back to my room and saw that the door across the hall was still open. No one would know if I went inside. I did, and I saw a study that looked much like my dad's at home. On Joe's desk was an open folder with pages of notes—I began to read them and then I turned away. I had never read patient files when I saw them at home. They dealt with a person's life and I wondered how Joe knew the same cryptic shorthand Dad would use. On top of the notes was a slip of paper with just three words.

I looked at the wall behind Joe's desk. I had not paid attention to it when I walked into his room before. Joe said he never completed his studies, and I thought he meant his Bachelor's, but he meant something beyond his Doctorate. I saw three diplomas on the wall, and I wondered if Joe had studied to be a psychiatrist like my dad. They had graduated from the same schools. And many of the books Joe had were also in Dad's library.

I tried to sleep but was awake long before breakfast. When Joe's truck appeared, I slipped out the front door. "Where's Mike? Is his brother going to be all right?"

Joe climbed the steps slowly. He seemed to have grown old in the hours he was gone. Joe finally said Mike was taking care of business.

"Can we help?" I asked. "Why didn't Mike go in the first place?"

Joe just looked at me and shook his head, "It's a long story. Jim's dying and George needs to be with them both." I stopped babbling and remembered the words that I'd seen on Joe's desk—deadly terminal cancer.

Mike didn't want a service at the church back home, but he said Gram and the rest of the family would be disappointed if he did nothing. I didn't understand why he thought curiosity seekers would show up to a funeral.

George said James had told him what he wanted, and Joe told both men that we'd help. After the decisions were made in town. Mike came back to work at the rodeo grounds. He worked all day but didn't rhyme anyone's name.

Before the first bull ride, I listened to the announcer introduce George and he talked about Mike's brother. He said he never left a cowboy alone in the dirt. He was a man everyone liked, but nobody really knew. The day Jim Bob painted his face—James Robert ceased to exist. All the bull riders nodded their heads in agreement.

From where I sat on Smokey Friday evening, I saw Mike come down from the chutes. Joe saw him too and asked me to keep an eye on him. I was glad Joe trusted me, but when I reached camp, I didn't know what I should say. Mike had never said he had a brother. He lifted the Windswept from Smokey and I exchanged the bridal for a halter before I spoke. "You didn't tell me you were brothers."

"That's okay. Not many knew. Some days I was able to forget who, and what he was."

"Your own brother," I questioned Mike. "I'm sure that didn't please your parents." I tied Smokey to the tether line and gave him a measure of grain.

I followed Mike to the fire circle, and he said, "It don't matter." He struck a match and dropped it into the kindling. The small sticks ignited and burned. "They're dead and buried." He added limb wood and then a log.

I reached out and told him—your brother saved people's lives.

"And he's the reason they died." I withdrew my hand and Mike kept talking. He pulled a gold chain and charm from his pocket. "Joe's dad had this made before he died. He gave it to James and said if he ever got hurt—someone would find us. That's how they found me yesterday, but I wouldn't go to my own brother." Tears ran down his cheeks. "George knows more about my brother than I ever did."

"He was sick," I told Mike, and tried to hug him.

"Yeah, sick in the head." Mike broke loose of my arms and stood up to face me.

73

"No!" I said. "He was really sick," but I didn't realize how sick. "I should have said something," I didn't know this was going to happen. *My mother would have known better.*

Mike said he wouldn't have listened, and James would have denied everything. Mike kissed my cheek. "You're a smart girl not to keep secrets." He left camp with his toiletries and when he returned, Mike said he thought James was peculiar, and he was stupid.

Joe came over to us and said James never blamed you Mike—but it is hard for those who are different. Joe spoke quietly, calming Mike's anger. "Maybe they will achieve the same freedoms we have some day—maybe not—but I hope they do. The choices we make shouldn't be an embarrassment or a problem to ourselves or anyone else."

Joe spoke in conundrums. My dad often did the same. I repeated Joe's words—the choice he made for himself. I wondered how choice had anything to do with Mike's brother.

As I walked away, George took my place at the fire—he had been gone all day. The piece of paper on Joe's desk referred to cause of death. There were only men working at the ranch and tonight I wondered if some of them could have been gay. I know that Dad counseled anyone who needed help. I remember him saying if someone was homosexual, they didn't really have any choice in the matter. The folder and notes I had seen on Joe's desk were mine. I wondered who else Joe had folders for. *What kind of secrets had the men working for Joe kept? Who or whom had they kept them from— and for how long?*

I was standing in the middle of our camp when Mike nodded in my direction. I heard him say, that I had more courage than any of them had. Mike said that he needed to forgive his brother, and he told Joe that he needed to talk about his wife.

I went to bed thinking about what Mike had said. I thought I should tell him that I had no more courage than any of them. I wasn't about to tell anyone what the rapist had made me do.

On Sunday morning, everyone packed their tents up. By the time Joe's stock had been fed, clouds had moved in. I hoped the rain would end before the afternoon performance.

I walked into town with everyone from the campground, and we went into an old stone church where the preacher talked about rodeo.

74

Joe stepped out from behind the podium and eulogized his friend—the rodeo clown named Jim Bob. As he talked, Joe said we were all obligated to help the man or woman beside us. He said that if you see someone in pain, you needed to help. The people around me listened to every word he said. "Take the chance of having someone tell you no and have your feelings hurt. The risk you take may save a life."

When the service was over, I stepped in front of Joe as we neared the rodeo grounds and asked how I could help him.

Joe looked at me and laughed, not realizing how serious I was in asking about him. He told me to go help Mike—we didn't have much time to get ready. Outside the arena, I saw Joe reach a hand around Tina's waist. "How's my girl?" he asked, and I listened to Tina say something that could have been scandalous. She asked Joe about a woman named Laurie and a baby.

I thought back to both nights when Joe had tried to leave me at Mrs. Montoya's home. Had he gotten someone pregnant in the past? Is that why he didn't want me—*a girl*—in his house. I quickly shook that thought from my mind. I didn't think Joe was that kind of a man. After I had been raped—he had been kind and tried to help me.

I had heard enough to know that I didn't want to be anywhere in sight when Joe came around the corner. Laurie and that baby—who was Tina talking about, I wondered—And what did Mike know about the woman in Joe's past?

Chapter 13

When the rodeo was over, the big rigs were loaded—and when they moved out—the arena was empty. I took a deep breath and turned to face my boss of just over a month. "I'm sorry if I've made things difficult for you. Should I go back to Oklahoma? Gram says you like to put families back together."

Joe looked at me with a puzzled look on his face. "What are you talking about?" He shook his head as I climbed the fence under the announcer's platform.

"I heard you and Tina talking."

Joe looked behind himself and asked where she was—and then he said I wasn't making any sense.

"Damn it all, stop talking—I'm trying to say something." I turned a half circle and hooked my heels over the second board of the fence. I held onto the fence at my back and looked into his eyes, "You can fire me if you want, but I gotta ask if you got someone pregnant?" Joe stood motionless with his mouth open and I chose my words carefully, "Did a girl named Laurie say you got her pregnant?"

Joe closed his eyes—he took a long, thin breath through pursed lips before he spoke. "Laurie was my wife's name," he whispered.

I said, "The baby," and held my breath.

"When Laurie left, I thought she was pregnant." Joe opened his eyes and looked at me. "But she never said there was a baby."

"Then how do you know if there ever was one?" I stepped off the fence and my hands dropped to my side.

"A lawyer sent papers to sign, and we were divorced."

How long ago I asked.

"Twenty-two years it is now."

"Is this what Mike was talking about last night?" We walked through the empty campground.

"If I have a son, he'd be about your age."

Joe stopped and I asked if that was why he wanted me to be a boy so bad. I watched Joe nod his head. "You don't know—she might not have been pregnant, or she could have had a girl. You really don't know if you have a son—or a daughter." I bit my lower lip, and finished my thought, "or neither."

Joe shook his head, "There was a child. I know it in my heart. I have a son."

I heard thunder and felt the ground vibrate beneath my feet. "We better get outta here."

Joe pulled his keys along with a clean handkerchief from his pocket. "Let's head for home." He wiped his eyes as I reached for my key.

Joe's engine started with a deafening roar, and he took the lead. At the main road, three big rigs fell in line behind me. With two blasts from an air horn, I heard a familiar voice. "We got her boxed in. Our little girl won't get lost."

I smiled to myself and thought, this is the Mike I like. My hat hung in the hat rack alone. I felt at home in this world of cowboys and rodeo. We were a family, and we cared about each other, but it wasn't quite the same as having Jen live next door.

As we drove, I could see heat lightning flash in the sky around us. When the sky opened in front of Joe, he warned us that the rain was going to hit us hard. Because I couldn't see around his double, he checked his mirrors to see that I drove at a safe distance, close enough to see his lights yet far enough behind to stop if he had a problem.

Mike pulled back. We didn't need to pile up—the two horses and I would never have a chance between Joe's double and Mike's own forty-footer.

"Chris, keep both hands on the wheel. We'll talk you through this. Don't worry about the radio." Joe's voice echoed in my cab.

"She's fine Joe, straight as an arrow," Mike answered for me as my fingers gripped the wheel. I'd never driven in rain this hard.

I remembered being at Niagara Falls. I'd gone into tunnels on the Canadian side. On Goat Island, I'd been soaked. I felt the gale force winds generated from the water hitting the rocks at the base of the falls.

I don't remember stopping, but we must have. Outside there was nothing but water. I pressed the gas pedal, but the truck didn't move. Dry and in the cab, I thought I was inside one of the contraptions people had used to go over the falls. I finally heard Mike say take your hands off the damn wheel and pick up the radio. His voice reverberated in the cab of my truck, and probably everyone else's on our frequency.

We should have made the drive in an hour; but with the rain it was closer to three. Bright yellow ponchos met us to unload the stock. Once unhooked from my trailer, I pulled up to Joe and told him I had to go back into town for something. He asked if I was sick and Mike got into the truck cab with me. He told Joe to be careful, or we'd send him to the drug store with a list.

Mike slipped into the driver's seat and turned the truck around while I was inside making my purchases. It was one of the few businesses allowed to be open on Sunday and they stayed open late. As I got back into the truck and pulled my door shut, everything spilled onto the seat. I was soaked and my bag had disintegrated from the rain. Mike said take your time and he asked if it was that time of the month? He nodded to the box wrapped in brown paper that had landed on the floor. His hands gripped the steering wheel, "I was afraid you might be pregnant."

I told Mike not to scare me any worse than I already was.

The rain stopped by morning and I looked for Jim's trailer. George had driven it home and said it was where Jim always tucked it in. He asked me to ride with him, and at the end of Joe's drive, we turned right and a quarter mile down the road we made another right. Pam and her parents lived in the home where Mike and his brother had grown up. Other than Gram, they were our closest neighbors. I saw the trailer beyond their house and George parked our truck nearby. The door of the camper faced the back of their house, and the awning was open.

George said we're early for the remembering. Many came to remember James and I listened to stories about Joe, James, and Michael when they were young.

Mike walked home with me down the middle of the road. Halfway to Joe's, he stopped, turned to face me and grabbed hold of my hand, "Chris, what I wanted to say last night—is that if you were pregnant, we have doctors that would help you." He squeezed my hand, "I just want you to know that."

"Let's hope I'm not."

* * *

In another week, Joe caught me looking at his desk calendar. I had my right index finger on that day's date and with my left hand, I was progressing backwards, one day at a time. Damn. It can't have been that long.

Joe came around the corner and asked what I was doing? I dropped my hands to my sides. "I'm late," I told Joe, but he didn't seem to understand. I blurted out, "It's been nearly six weeks. I might be pregnant." He grabbed at my hand—took me through the house and pulled me out the front door.

I asked where we were going and he said, "Away from ears that might be listening." Joe said that if I was pregnant, how *we* dealt with it—was our decision, no one else's.

I whirled around to face Joe, "This isn't your decision—this isn't *our* problem," Joe closed the pasture gate. "It's my problem—and I have to decide what to do about it."

Joe looked at me and quietly said, "You can have the baby and give the child up—or raise it yourself."

I didn't answer Joe. He had no idea what had happened to me— or how I felt about it. I walked away from Joe and then I turned to face him. "I don't want to be pregnant. Mike said doctors could help me—if I were."

Joe shook his head, "If you are pregnant, you're carrying a life inside of you." Joe said that he would marry me—I could have the baby, and he would divorce me quietly. I would be free to go on with my life as if nothing had ever happened. He would raise my child, as Laurie raised his, alone.

That was twenty some years ago I told him. "It's not right to take my baby and raise it as yours because you think Laurie was pregnant. You don't know if she was—just like I don't know if I am." I walked in circles, verbally reciting all the options available to me. I stopped to face Joe—when I experienced pain in my gut—I grabbed for my stomach and when I could breathe, I stood up straight. Then just as quickly—I doubled over and saw the ground come rushing at me. Joe scooped me into his arms. Mike saw what was happening and he opened gates and doors for us. He grabbed a towel and put it on my bed before Joe laid me down. I rolled away from them my shorts all covered in blood.

Mike found an unopened bottle of pills on my dresser and removed the wad of cotton. He helped me to sit on the edge of my bed and placed two pills in my hand, I looked at them and asked—how he knew what I needed. He winked at me when he gave me a glass of water. "I've known Dr. Grace a long time and she's taught me a lot." When the pain subsided, I selected clean underwear and a pair of jeans. Mike un-wrapped the box from the drugstore and gave me a pad on my way to the bathroom.

Joe argued with Mike and I cried out when there was another contraction. Mike opened the door and came to me. He lifted me into his arms and said he was taking me to see Dr. Grace. I rested my head on his shoulder, and at the clinic Mike answered all of Grace's questions. He really did know a lot—about what was happening to me and to my body.

Dr. Grace tried to send both men out of the room, and I said, "No!" She covered me with a sheet before she removed my jeans and underwear. She said the pain would soon be nothing more than a bad memory.

Mike held my hand and tried to distract me. Grace's hands were as cold as ice when she guided my feet into metal stirrups attached to her table. I'm glad she had left my socks on. I remembered the rapist spreading my legs apart and I held my breath. Mike gently tapped my face with his fingers until I remembered to breathe.

Dr. Grace sat at the end of her exam table and pushed in the shelf she had pulled out to support my legs—they were in the air and a sheet covered them. She wiped the bloody discharge that kept coming from inside me as she talked. "Many women abort and never know anything is happening except for the cramping and heavy flow.

81

You're going to feel a sucking sensation, but I promise—this won't hurt." I felt something cold and slippery slide inside me. I heard a motor hum and felt Grace's cold hand on my stomach. And then something warm took its place. Joe was watching my face, but his body was behind the sheet that hid Dr. Grace from my view. I closed my eyes and felt the warmth and pressure of Joe's hand on my stomach. It felt as if he was kneading bread dough before allowing it to rise. When the pressure was gone, I opened my eyes to see that Joe had turned his back to me.

I felt a warm, wet cloth between my legs. Grace reached for a dry towel and then removed my feet from the stirrups and guided each one into my panties with a clean pad in place.

Mike helped me to sit up. He held my jeans open so I could slip both feet down the legs at the same time. When I stood—the sheet covering me fell to the floor. Grace picked it up and covered the soiled towels and instruments with it when I put my boots on.

Joe looked back when we left the exam room, which made me wonder what he was thinking. Could his baby have died? Was that why Laurie had left so many years before, or had she left to end the pregnancy? I wondered why Joe had never been told if he had a child or not? Not knowing what had happened made me feel sorry for him.

That afternoon, I was in the field with Smokey when Joe came to my side. I told him I wasn't trying to be mean when I asked if his wife lost his baby or maybe she wasn't even pregnant. I told Joe that whatever reason his wife had for not telling him about their child, I didn't think it was right. I looked up at Joe and said—I'm glad I'm not pregnant because I didn't want the rapist's baby, but now I feel empty.

Joe shook his head, "You didn't do anything to make your baby die—and I know you have a hole inside of you with nothing to make the emptiness go away. I could never explain that feeling to anyone," Joe leaned back to the fence rail and looked up to the sky. "I thought no one would or even could understand how I felt." In a little while— Joe asked what I remembered about my father.

I shook my head and told him I didn't remember anything because he died before I was born.

"Do you think Laurie has told my son that I died—so she wouldn't have to explain my absence?"

I reached out to touch Joe's arm, "Mom and Dad have told me about my father. I know who he was." I wasn't sure what else I could say to make Joe feel better, but I told him—I still have a good friend, even though I don't know where Jen is now—or if I'll ever see her again. Joe took a deep breath and nodded. I saw a tear in the corner of his eye and thought I had said the right thing about knowing how he felt.

Chapter 14

Tom blocked the hallway where we all hung our outside gear and left muddy boots. He was watching John twirl his shaving brush in a stream of hot water at the mudroom sink. Neither one had seen me come into the kitchen for a cookie.

John touched the wet brush to the cake of hard soap in the ceramic mug he held. Like whipped cream, lather appeared when he made circles with his brush. Tom asked, do you know what happened to Chris as I poured myself some milk.

John tipped and turned his head to see that lather covered his entire face. There were mirrors on three sides of the mudroom sink and I could see his reflection in one of them. "She was at Gram's for lunch." John grinned as he wiped the excess lather from his lips. He set the mug down to reach for his razor. "Did you set up another practical joke for her?"

"I didn't do nothin', but Joe carried her into the house from the front field. Not long after that, he and Mike left with her. I thought you might know if she had gotten hurt." Tom continued to watch John bring the straight razor from below his collar line to his chin— stretching his neck taut. "They both fuss over her."

Rinsing the blade, John spoke, "I saw her come across the field this afternoon. But I don't think she rode today," The lather had all but gone from his face.

"If she didn't ride, something's wrong," Tom said.

"Yo, John," Mike came in from outside, interrupting their conversation. "Is anybody going to be at the house tonight?" Mike's body filled what was left of the hallway.

John said he had plans and asked about me. Mike just said I should be resting, and I left my empty glass on the counter. John dropped his razor and lunged at Mike. "She didn't try to hurt herself, did she?"

Mike turned to steady him. "She's fine. I just don't want her to be alone while some of us go into town."

"So now she needs a babysitter," Tom said sarcastically. John went back to the sink and scooped water onto his face. "Don't worry about Chris. I'll stick around the house tonight." Tom picked up a towel and handed it to John.

Mike saw me leave the kitchen but didn't say anything to the others. He brought a plate of food to my room before dinner and sat with me while I ate.

When I thought they had all gone for the evening, I came out of my room. Tom looked up from the paper he was reading and said he missed me at dinner.

"I wasn't very hungry," I told him. "Maybe I should go home now. You could say you ran me off." I sat down in one of the stuffed chairs near him.

Tom came over to stand and then squat in front of me, "What's wrong?" he asked.

I didn't know why I suggested leaving the ranch. Tom was accepting of my help on days he cooked. I would dust and add apples to the roasters. "This place wouldn't be the same without you," I flinched when he placed a hand on my thigh to steady himself. "You need to bake your apples with cinnamon candies when I do a roast this week."

I thought for a moment and asked what he knew about Cuervo. The phone rang before he had a chance to answer. Tom pushed on my leg and I flinched again. He did a quick shake of his head, when he said, "Engelmann ranch." Tom listened to the voice on the other end of the phone line. "I'll let her speak for herself," and he brought the phone to me. "Doctor Grace is asking about you."

Tom went back to the paper he had been reading, and I told Grace there had been no more pain and discomfort. After I said goodbye, Tom put the phone back on Joe's desk.

"I hear she's a good doctor." He came back to squat in front of me. "You know, I've been thinking about when I was your age."

I smiled, "You're not that much older than me."

"I know," Tom nodded. "I was just thinking that I sowed some pretty wild oats and got myself into trouble when I was younger. I had lots of girlfriends." And then he asked if I was pregnant. I answered him truthfully, shaking my head from side to side.

Tom reached for my hands and I pulled them away. I stood up and knocked him off balance. "I'll be in my room." He followed me, and I told him you're not allowed back here.

Tom ignored me and picked up a blanket from my bed. He forcefully pushed me back into the front room. "I think you need some company tonight." Tom placed the blanket over the back of the couch before he sat down. "I won't bite," he said when he took a pillow and positioned it in his lap. Following his silent commands—I sat down beside him—stretched out—and laid my head on the pillow. Tom looked down at me and grinned. "You like being a bratty little sister." He pulled the blanket over me and rubbed my shoulder. I pulled my knees up to my stomach and tried to hug myself.

I took a deep breath and expelled it slowly. I said my baby died this morning and I buried my face in the pillow on Tom's lap.

Tom's hand felt heavy on my shoulder when he said—now he understood why they didn't want me left alone. Tom reached behind the couch and turned off the floor lamp. He touched my hair in the dark and asked, what else had happened to me.

I said nothing but felt my body spasm beneath the blanket. I wondered if Tom had ever asked—or forced a girl to do the things done to me. *After all, he was one of the boys.* I had heard him talking before my rape—when he and others didn't think I was listening. They had often discussed girls that they knew and their reputations. And I remembered the men talking the night Joe didn't want me in the house. Since then I hadn't heard any of them—speak disrespectfully about any woman.

One by one, everyone returned home. George thought I should see a doctor as he stood in front of the couch. Tom told him I had. When John knelt and said I hope the rapist that did this—rots in hell— I knew I had no secrets. I told Tom I had lost my baby today and I was sure he would tell the others.

Eventually, I stood up and looked at all the men in the room with me. I said I felt safe and protected with all of them in this house and on the road.

I walked toward my room and I was just out of their sight when Tom said, "She belongs here like the rest of us. I think her scars—run pretty deep from what she's been through." He hesitated, and then said, "The way we were raised was wrong. And only we can change the culture—to become better sons and fathers."

I think that maybe he had done things—that he wasn't very proud of now.

Chapter 15

One day in July, I looked up to see Tom go into Joe's private study and shut the door. I checked my watch. The dryer still had twenty minutes to go, and I felt uncomfortable being in my own room.

I found out later that Joe arranged for Tom to go home and visit his family. A week after that, I wrote on the board—

> 2:00—Tom called.
>
> Gone to pick him up in town
>
> and bring him home
>
> —Chris

I looked for someone to go with me, but everyone was away from the house. I pulled a set of keys from the board and looked around again before I got into the blue beast. The engine purred like a kitten. Just as I released the clutch, bright flashes of light distorted my vision—*God not now.* The truck rolled backwards out of its parking spot. My foot moved to the brake pedal and I slammed it into the floorboard. I put the truck in gear, set the parking brake and turned off the motor.

I laid my forehead on the steering wheel just as George appeared at my door. "You almost hit me!" He yelled as he reached past the steering column and took the key from the ignition switch.

"Aw, come on! I didn't hit you."

"Where do you think you're going?"

"I gotta pick Tom up at the bus station coz he just called."

"Get out." George opened my door and waited. When I didn't move, he pulled me off the seat and slipped into it himself. "I'll stop for ice cream if you want to ride along."

He waited for me to walk around the truck and I knew he was right in pulling me from behind the wheel. I was experiencing an optical migraine and I was afraid that it could be a precursor to more problems. I never knew how long it would be—until I'd be able to see clearly. At times it was only a few seconds, and then there were other times I couldn't see clearly for minutes.

George stopped at the ice cream stand. He brought two cones wrapped in paper napkins back to the truck. I wasn't going to drive, I told him. I set the brake, put the truck in gear, and turned off the motor. I felt the melting ice cream touch my hand and I began to lick the cold treat.

George thought Doc Williams should look at my eyes, but I told him Tom was waiting on us, and he was anxious to get back to the ranch. *I didn't think doc would be able to help if something was wrong. He was just a G.P.*

Joe was at our mailbox and had the mail in his hand when George turned into the drive. Joe asked Tom how the trip had been as he stepped out of the pickup truck.

"I should have apologized long before now. I was pretty disrespectful to my step-mom and her daughters when I left home."

"Or maybe you just needed time to grow up," Joe said, as the two men walked to the house.

George parked at the split in the drive. With truck keys in hand, he placed Tom's bags near the front door. George returned and asked me for my license. I begged him not to take it, saying that I wouldn't try to drive again.

I went into the house by way of the mudroom. From the living room, I heard Tom ask if I was all right. "I'm perfectly fine," I said coming through the room to the front door. I separated the men, giving each one a push with my open hand.

Tom caught—and held onto my hand. "Are you two fighting already?" Joe asked as he looked up from the mail.

"I haven't told anyone your baby died," Tom whispered. And then he let go of my hand.

90

George said he'd keep a close eye on me, and Joe asked if either man thought there was a reason for concern as I left the house. George said, she's our girl and we need to see that no harm comes to her.

Everywhere we went Joe bought newspapers. Gram had been clipping articles about Joe and his stock for years. The night we finished mounting the clippings in scrapbooks, my eyes were so strained that I felt like digging them out of their sockets. I'd even been wearing my glasses. I tried not to worry, but I could never forget about my eyes.

Gram said I should take the books home and that we'd start another next week and not let the clippings pile up. I kept turning my head so I could see where I was going. Bright lights were flashing again today, and I was scared my retina could once again detach. I followed the drive around the house to the kitchen. As I walked between the mudroom and laundry, the fireworks behind my eyelids diminished. When I reached the living room, I could see someone sitting on the couch and a head bobbed behind the newspaper. I crossed the room and stood in front of Joe. I bent down so I knew I had the coffee table in front of me and then I allowed the photo albums to drop.

The sound startled Joe. He put the paper down and looked through the albums. As he did, I thought about the events surrounding the early summer. Joe had relaxed. He'd seen me embrace Mike, John, and even Tom. I had been adamant from the beginning that he could have had a daughter and I felt a tear spill out of my eye.

Joe stood and touched my cheek. He asked me what was wrong. I turned away muttering something about it having been a long day, but Joe moved with me and caught my chin in his hand. "Look at me! What's wrong with your eye?"

I tried to move away but his grip on my chin was firm. "My eyes are just fine." I had to pry his hand from my face.

He told me my eye looked irritated and I should see Doc Williams.

"No," I snapped. "If there was something wrong, I'd know it." I moved around the room like a cat. "It's just eyestrain."

Joe looked back at the scrapbooks, "You could be right, if you've read all those articles."

Chapter 16

Fall was fast approaching and I—I alone—would represent Horse Springs in Albuquerque on Saturday. It would be my chance to show off, and I wanted to win.

I thought riding in the truck with Mike would be safe because he hadn't said anything about my eyes, but I was mistaken. He asked what my problem was before we got two miles from home. Mike reached over and touched my shoulder, "You haven't been at the ranch for very long, but I hope you realize—"

"I wouldn't have made it through the summer without you and the others," I said.

When he asked why I wouldn't tell him what was wrong, I just stared stonily at the road ahead.

When we got to Albuquerque, my past continued to haunt me. I knew I could get hurt, but I didn't want to tell anyone my vision was decreasing by the hour, and that I was afraid I would soon be blind again. I took my time to secure the gate to the stock pens. When I turned around, I literally ran into Joe. He steadied me and gripped my shoulders with both his hands—saying we should find an ophthalmologist to check my eyes while we're in town. I brought my hands up, between his, and pushed his hands away.

"What's the chip on your shoulder?" Joe was annoyed with me and he had every right to be.

"You like to see Tina win!" I brushed some imaginary dirt off my pants, so he wouldn't see my tears. I wanted to scream, and I guess I did. "No matter how hard I work, she always wins. Maybe, just some time, don't you think, I'd like to come in first."

Joe realized I was mad, but most of all—*I was scared.*

I walked away and when I reached the tree line near our camp, I could feel the coolness of the shade and I leaned against a tree. My eyes had adjusted by the time I got back to camp.

Albuquerque was a long rodeo. Our crew would change twice, and all the drivers would be there for the weekends. We didn't need all the trucks, as there were several stock contractors and that made it easier for me to avoid driving.

At noon on Saturday, I dressed in the darkened trailer and allowed Smokey to pick our way to the arena. My reins hung loose over the saddle horn during the Grand Entry. I found a spot to sit on the fence and threaded Smokey's reins over my belt to wait my turn. I could hear the rodeo—I smelled it—and I tasted it. I walked Smokey to the gate where we would enter when it was time for the barrels.

Tina rode up behind me and wished me luck—but at that moment in time, I didn't want to hear anything she had to say. My mind was somewhere else.

> For me—that day, life at the ranch was about to take a crucial turn—a turn that would profoundly change my existence and Joe's—for all of eternity. Seconds evolved into minutes, and minutes would turn into hours—hours into days—and days would become weeks.

When I rode into the arena, I was busy thinking that I might have a chance if the lowering shade in my eye would only stop. I didn't hear the announcer speak about me, my accomplishments, and the fact that I came from Horse Springs. I backed into one of the boxes, leaned forward, touched my horse, and grabbed the pommel of my saddle— I urged Smokey with my voice, my hands, and my legs. The windswept held me tight. I knew I could reach out and touch the ground with my hand as we circled each barrel in a cloud of dust— Did I remember my "ho" and "hup" commands? It didn't matter. Smokey knew when to move, how close he could come, and how far he could lean without touching the barrel. His rooster tail was flying three feet back when we nearly ran through the wooden gate.

The gatekeeper was slow. Smokey side stepped at the last moment. He took his cool down circle inside the arena while the announcer shouted over the roar of the crowd. He said my time was seconds faster than anyone had done for a long time. I had set an arena record.

Tears streamed down my cheeks as I felt the ground shake from the stomping of boots in the stands. I turned to the sound of Joe's distinctive whistle. I raised my hands to the sky and acknowledged the victory I had so dearly coveted.

I wiped tears from my face, and Mike said my practice had paid off. He touched my elbow and helped me to dismount. "I'll walk Smokey out and take him back to camp." In a matter of seconds, I stood alone in the crowd of working cowboys behind the chutes.

I heard a strange, yet familiar voice—call out my name. A man appeared beside me and asked if I was from Horse Springs. I said that I was.

"Ha-have you lived there very long?" The stranger in front of me seemed to stutter.

"I've only been there for the summer." I wanted to call home, but this stranger was talking to me.

I focused on the man near me. He towered over me, but I couldn't tell if he was young or old.

He realized I was distracted and said, "I'm sorry. I shouldn't have bothered you."

I told him it was all right, and I stumbled on my own words. I took a deep breath and the oxygen cleared my mind. "It sounds like you have a question—but I have no idea what it might be."

"I'm looking for someone—but I don't think you've lived there long enough to know everyone in town." He sounded disappointed and yet I was surprised that his voice had a calming effect on me.

"Wait," I said as I reached out to his voice. He had begun to walk away, "I work for one of the stock contractors." Our hands touched. His skin was smooth, no callouses. He wasn't a cowboy. "I'm sure my boss would know who you're looking for. He's old enough to be my father, and he spent his whole life in Horse Springs. What's your name? You seem to know mine."

"Most people call me Alex. That's short for Alexander. Close friends call me AJ."

I told Alex I'd like to get away from the crowd to make a phone call. He saw a phone and guided me to it. "You must be proud," he said, and I reminded him he hadn't told me yet—who he was looking for.

That's right, I haven't, he said as we walked. I'm looking for a man named Joseph—and at that moment, Bob Mason interrupted and said, "Great ride." I acknowledged the compliment and I heard Tina's mare whinny as they walked away. Neither one had paid any attention to the man between us. I concentrated on AJ—Alex, like Joseph, seemed so formal. "I work for Joe, but I've never heard him talk about a Joseph, not even referring to himself. The boss is just Joe."

AJ picked up the receiver from the telephone pole and handed it to me. He pulled change from his pocket and said, "I'll put a dime in and if you need privacy I'll leave." I didn't answer AJ on the privacy question as we never had very much at the ranch, and there was definitely no privacy at the rodeos.

I still wasn't sure who he was looking for as I followed the cord from the handset to the pole. Joseph was just a first name and I dialed the operator. I gave my parents' phone number and I forgot that AJ was close enough to hear my conversation.

Dad said he would accept the charges and he asked me what was wrong. He reached for his pen and a piece of paper. He always seemed to do that, I thought. In fact—I don't think I ever saw Dad answer the phone without a pen in his hand and a paper nearby. I said, "I'm scared." He thought I was hurt, and I repeated myself, "I'm scared," my voice rising in pitch.

Dad asked me why and he tried to remain calm.

"I'm seeing bright lights like before when the doctor said it was a migraine inside my eye. Only now I'm sure my retina is detaching."

Dad asked where I was, and he would have written Albuquerque on the blank page. He told me later that he did. He asked what I could see, and I said, "It's like a gate dropping down in front of me. The gate stops, and then it goes back up." I walked around the pole as far as the cord would allow me to go and reversed my direction.

Dad tried to tell me I needed to see an ophthalmologist, but I reminded him it was Saturday afternoon. That's when Dad told me, I'll drive to Albuquerque and fetch you home.

95

"No!" I cried out, "I am at home. I mean I'm home away from home when I'm not at the ranch." My tongue was all tied up in knots.

Alex stepped up to my side when I hung up the receiver. "You shouldn't be here alone. Maybe you should be the one talking to your boss," and he grabbed hold of my hand.

The PA system clicked. "Shush," I hissed. The announcer's voice called for me to come to the chute area.

Alex tugged at my hand and said, "I'll walk you over."

When we neared the chutes, George called out my name and I nearly jumped out of my skin when he grabbed my arm. He wasn't gentle about it, and he steered us through the crowd to the announcer's booth.

I heard Mike yell George has her, and I smelled his aftershave as he came close to us.

There were people all around, and I tried to tell Mike that AJ was looking for someone, but he wouldn't let me talk.

Mike told George to stay with me and to wait for Joe. "I'll take care of this," Mike said as he separated me from Alex. Alex disappeared along with the smell of Mike's aftershave.

When Joe got to my side, George told those within earshot that I should see a doctor, 'cause maybe I needed an operation.

I turned on him, "How do you know what I need?"

"Settle down," Joe said as he took hold of my wrist. What's wrong with you? He ushered me away from the crowd and put a clean handkerchief in my hand so I could clean the bubbles of snot coming from my nose. "We'll find you a doctor, don't worry."

Chapter 17

I agreed to go to the hospital. I knew I had to—if I were to get any sight back. I was afraid I could become totally blind, but I don't think Joe understood what that meant. I didn't think anybody could—unless they were in my shoes. I had been legally blind in one eye for years. The term legally, didn't mean I couldn't see anything. I could see light and I could see shadows. In reality, I was only partially blind. If I took my time and paid attention, I could figure out what was in front of me. Like the E on the eye chart, I could see it at twenty feet, but at thirty it disappeared. When I could see, it was clear at two hundred feet.

I waited in the truck while Joe unhooked the camper. Mike came to stand beside my open window. He said he knew about the man Alex wanted to find and told me he'd come find me later.

I had forgotten about Alex in that short time and I forgot about him again when Joe took me into the emergency room. The antiseptic smell turned my stomach and I was glad when a doctor sent me to the eye building. Once I got there, some of my past came rushing back to me. I couldn't read anything on the eye chart except for the E, and even that was difficult with what had been my *good* eye, the only eye that I had been able to see with for a couple years now.

Dr. Burke took me downstairs for tests. He wouldn't let me leave the hospital and said he would review my case overnight. He told me that my retina was detaching, and there were other things happening inside my eye. He stressed that if I wanted to see, he would have to operate and do it soon.

When Dr. Burke placed drops in my eye, I told him he'd had the bottles in his pant's pockets, and not in his white coat.

He asked me how I knew, and I said—because the drops were warm. They flowed over the surface of my eye—and out onto my face.

He said the next time they'd be cold, and I'd feel the drop splash in my eye.

A nurse named Jane gave me a Kleenex and she made Joe leave my room when the doctor left. I asked Joe to call my parents—so they would know what was happening. I got undressed, and the nurse did the prep work for my operation. By the time Mike got to my room, Nurse Jane had finished with me. When she left, she made sure the door was propped open.

From my bed I heard Mike tell Joe to find the chapel and say some prayers for me. Mike came into my room and held my hand. He told me to think good thoughts and he was sure that I'd be just fine.

I heard footsteps stop in the hall just outside my room. I thought it was Joe, but then I realized that if it had been him—he'd have come in and asked if I behaved myself while he was gone. I sent Mike out to see who was in the hall. He squeezed my hand as he got to his feet and when he was near the door, He said, "I thought you'd left." I didn't hear an answer, but when Mike came back to my side, he brought someone with him.

Alex took my hand and held it tightly. I said, "I wish I could say that I remembered your name—but I'm sorry—I don't."

It's AJ—Alex said. "You were preoccupied earlier today, and now I hear that they've scheduled you for surgery."

"That's right," Mike answered for me.

"Then allow me to wish you the best of luck, and I'll let you get some rest."

All of a sudden—I remembered that Alex was looking for someone named Joseph. I asked if he had found him yet and I thought I could see Mike shaking his head from side to side.

"Mike here, he was able to point me in the right direction."

"But I'd like to help too, if I could," I said.

There were more footsteps, and then Joe's voice, "You should be resting." Joe came around my bed and he faced Alex.

99

Mike leaned over my face, "It's time you close your baby blues."

"Mike's right, you've got a big day tomorrow." It was Joe's voice. I looked from Joe to Alex and back again. They were standing on either side of my bed. I reached out and grabbed hold of their hands. I couldn't see either man clearly, but I was sure—Alex had to be Joe's son—both men were tall, their hands were the same size and I swear they sounded alike.

I stared at Alex and said you should tell the truth. He took a deep breath and I asked him—What's your name—who are you looking for?

"My name is Alexander Joseph Engelmann, AJ for short." I turned my head to look at Joe, but I don't think either man was paying any attention to me as I listened to AJ continue, "I'm looking for my father, and I believe you're him."

"You were right," I whispered, "You did have a son and now, he's right in front of you."

Joe released my hand and walked around the foot of my bed. He faced the young man and said, "Laurie gave you my name, but how did you find me?"

"She gave Alex the tools." Mike said quietly. "I took one look at the boy and knew you had been right for all these years."

I began to hyperventilate. Alex touched my hand and said, please relax and then he spoke to his father, "You never knew I existed, but yet—you knew—your thoughts have been with me every day of my life."

From the hallway Nurse Jane interrupted the reunion. The short, stocky nurse came into my room with her hands on her hips. She sent Mike and Alex away and put more drops into my eyes.

When I was alone with Joe, he held my hand next to his face. "I knew," he said, "I always knew there had been a child—and yet, if it hadn't been for you, a girl named Chris—I might never have met my son." Joe kissed my hand and I drifted off into my own world of dreams.

Chapter 18

As I slept in the hospital, my parents drove. They made their early morning appointment with Doctor Burke, and he brought them into my room.

Joe stepped away from my side and Dr. Burke left with him.

I didn't have very much time with my parents before two orderlies moved around my bed. When my bed moved, I realized they were taking me to surgery. My voice shattered the silence of the early morning hour, "No"— and I sat up. "Not yet!" I yelled. "You can't take me yet." My parents stepped up to either side of my bed, and I felt it stop.

"Chris," Dr. Burke said from outside my door. "We are taking you to surgery. Your parents and this cowboy can come with you."

Joe reached out and touched my arm. Mom squeezed my hand, and Dad kissed my forehead and helped me to lie back in my bed.

Dr. Burke finished pulling my bed into the hallway. He pushed it into the elevator and down another hall. He paused long enough to turn on lights as he went. "Chris, your family can stay with you until we get you under. While I operate, they'll have to stay outside, but I promise you this—nobody's going to leave."

I counted backwards—and then there was nothing. I don't remember how long, if anyone had told me, the surgery would take. I was shivering and heard someone say to get Chris a blanket. My surgeon said he couldn't operate in my eye if I couldn't stay still. He asked if anyone had been to Saturday's rodeo.

I remembered riding into the arena and when I left someone said I had done a good job and was taking the buckle home. Or did they say,

"Let's put the buckle in now?" And then there was nothing. I would have to ask my surgeon what they talked about during the operation.

They woke me up and helped me to turn over. I felt a cold chill and a warm blanket was placed over my shoulders. I fell asleep and when I heard Mom humming beside me, I realized I was back in my room. "It's over Chris—your doctor has done everything he could do—now it's your job to heal."

"Don't try to say anything—just rest," Dad said.

"We're still here Chris, and we won't go anywhere." I recognized Joe's voice and then I did rest. All day long I rested, and every time I started to wake up—I would hear voices—I would listen to them until I fell asleep—and woke up again.

Joe told my dad that he believed in miracles and Dad said he felt a peaceful calm come over him when Joe knelt in the chapel to pray.

"And I believe you have said prayers for my mother and I," Alex spoke from the door of my room.

"Is this your son?" Mom asked as she got up from the chair beside me.

"I'm sorry for interrupting." AJ's voice was coming directly to me. "I'm Alex Engelmann. I just wanted to check on Chris."

"Why don't you join the men?" Mom said. "And all of you—step outside for a minute. I want to help Chris with her gown."

Dad, Joe, and Alex stood in the hall to talk. I could hear their voices as Mom pulled my covers off. She helped me to turn over and sit up in my bed. Mom had me put on a second gown like a robe and she put pillows behind my back. "I think you'll feel more comfortable now—when your friends come to visit."

Those who were in the hall—came back inside my room. When Mike came—I smelled his aftershave when he stepped up to my bed and touched my cheek. When the doctor came, Mike asked what we had to do so I could work on my gold buckle next year. He said I had to compete, starting in January.

I wanted to look at the faces surrounding my bed, but I knew I shouldn't. The surgeon had placed a shield over my eye to protect it. He used five or six long pieces of tape to hold it in place. "Do you think I'll see to ride again?" I didn't like the tape touching my nose and I tried to get it loose.

Mike said if yesterday was an indicator of my ability—I had one hell of a chance to make it. He was ready to bet money on me.

Dr. Burke had used a gas bubble to keep my retina in place. But for the next three weeks, he said I had to look at my feet—twenty-four seven. Joe did the math—six hundred and seventy-two hours, six—six—six, and another six to boot.

The doctor said he put a buckle in my eye, but not the kind he thought I wanted. I tried to laugh. But I wasn't very happy. Dr. Burke said I shouldn't worry. I felt his fingers on my face and then a cold piece of metal cut the loose tape away. "Tomorrow, you can put the shield in place yourself." He went on to say it would take a long time for the swelling to go down so light could reach the back of my eye.

The surgeon kept me in the hospital for two more days. When Mike came, he brought rodeo food. Alex stopped on his way to work, over lunch, and at the end of his day. He had come to work and study in the physical therapy department while trying to decide between surgery or therapy for his career. AJ told Joe that he picked Albuquerque because it would get him close to Horse Springs. He apologized that he hadn't yet taken the time to search for his father.

A steady stream of people from the rodeo came to check on me. They didn't stay long, but I was glad they came. Joe came each night. He'd sleep in the chair beside me and he would go with me to see my surgeon in the morning. Mom came with us too and then she would stay all day.

Dad went home Monday and back to work on Tuesday. He had patients to see.

When Mom thought I was sleeping, I'd hear her talk to Joe and my nurses. She wanted to take me home to Oklahoma, but the doctor said, "Not yet. If Chris is going to get her sight back, we must come up with a plan that I believe she'll be able to live with. Otherwise I'll have to bring her back and put her in restraints."

"You don't want to do that," Joe told my surgeon.

Dr. Burke said he didn't want to do it to his staff, but he would if it meant that he could get some of my sight back for me. He said I been dealt a hand he wouldn't wish on anyone.

Mom must have looked at them both, and said, my daughter will play this hand and she will win!

"And I want her to win—don't get the wrong idea. She needs to go after that gold buckle. That's why I offered her my dictation services—so she could continue to journal."

For some reason Mom decided that she needed to talk to Dad—right then and—right there. She left Joe and my doctor alone at the door of my room, and I heard Joe say, "I think Chris's best chance would be with the men at my ranch. But if you think she should go to Oklahoma with her parents, George could get her there safely."

I listened to Dr. Burke ask if there was something Joe needed to tell him. Or as he put it, "It looks as if you need to get something off of your chest."

Very quietly Joe said something bad had happened—because he left me alone—and he wouldn't ever do that again. *I think Joe told my eye surgeon that I had been raped.* Joe's voice got louder when he said I'd get what I needed whether it was here or on the moon.

When Mom came back, Joe tried to tell her that she could bring me to the ranch when the Doctor allowed me to leave Albuquerque.

"I'll take care of my daughter," Mom said as she faced Joe. "I'll decide when Chris returns to your ranch."

"When might that be?" I heard sarcasm in Joe's voice, "Never?"

Mom seemed angry when she said, "Don't you put words in my mouth." I think she covered her mouth, because when she spoke again, her voice was muffled, "If Chris goes home with you, she's going to the next rodeo. You won't be able to stop her, and if you don't allow it, there's no telling what she'll do without you at the ranch."

I listened to Joe say he had invited my entire family. He didn't want to take me away from my parents, but Mom was frustrated, and she told Joe that she needed me at home. She said that it was important because she and my dad were moving. Mom said that she needed me to make decisions about all the things I had left behind.

Joe asked where are you moving? Mom said, "Gregg has taken a job in Silver City. When he interviewed over the summer we stopped at your place, but no one was home."

"Did you meet Gram?"

"Yes, she told us how busy life at the ranch was over the summer, and she suggested we just show up on your doorstep and drop off Chris's stuff."

"Women," Joe said shaking his head. "You like to conspire."

"I didn't want to do that. But now—being at home and going through her things will be good for Chris."

Chapter 19

On Wednesday I listened to my mother tell Joe that he reminded her of both—my father Geoff, as well as my dad Gregg. She told Joe that she liked Alex too, but that he was walking a fine line between his mother and father.

Joe said his wife raised a man he was proud to call his son.

Dr. Burke finally released me but said I could only go as far as AJ's apartment. When I left the hospital, I carried two clear plastic bags. One was filled with bottles of eye drops, and stuff for my eye, the second held my surgeon's tape recorder.

As soon as I got inside AJ's apartment, Mom showed me where my room was, and I quickly took the recorder out of its bag. I pressed the double button to record and began speaking—when I close my eyes, I see myself on Smokey. One more breath and I lean forward. Smoke and I are flying. My face is buried in his mane. Seconds pass. I have no intention of slowing down. I feel my leg brush the wood of the gate as we leave the arena—I talked into the recorder for so long after dinner that my tongue was sticking to the roof of my mouth and my lips. I needed water, and I wanted a big glass. I put the recorder down and tried to remember where the kitchen was. If I followed the hallway—I would eventually get to the living room.

I heard the east coast late night shows on the television when I started walking and thought Alex must still be awake and watching. We never took the time to watch them at the ranch. When I got to the end of the hallway, the sound of the television was gone. If Alex was still in the room, he didn't say anything.

I went a few steps further and felt the wall on my left end. I turned and with my left hand felt the stove. I extended my right hand out, and I was able to grab ahold of the refrigerator door. I took a deep breath—took one step—then another. With two more steps I had run into a counter. I touched the edge and found the sink. I thought to myself the glasses should be in a cabinet to my right or left. I found them and I ran the water until it was cold. With one of my fingers on the top edge of my glass, I filled but didn't overfill it. I was proud of myself. I brought the glass to my lips and I stopped. I couldn't lift or tilt my head backwards to drink from the glass. I used my tongue and slurped water into my mouth.

AJ cleared his throat, "Why don't you open the drawer to your right. I think you'll find what you need." I realized that he had been watching me. I found the drawer and pulled it open. Carefully, I reached inside. I found a silverware divider, and between it and the side of the drawer, I found straws wrapped in paper. I drank the whole glass of water and filled it again. "Don't you have to work tomorrow?" I asked, turning to where I'd heard AJ's voice.

"I'm off 'til noon. Do you want to sit with me until you get tired enough to go to bed?"

I took a step in his direction and asked, "Is there anything I can trip over?" AJ walked over to me and touched my hand. He guided me to the couch, and I asked him to tell me about himself. "All I really know is your name, and that you're Joe's son."

"And that's about all there is to know. I think your life is more interesting than mine."

"I don't think your dad would agree." I told AJ about Joe and I asked about his mother.

Alex said he remembered when he was only three or four, he would crawl into bed with his mother and she would hold him. AJ said his mom always told him they were going to be just fine, the two of them. I asked if she married again and AJ said no. "It's just the two of us and if I move away, she'll be alone. But if I move away— she might encourage her photographer friend to come around more often, or she'll travel with him. What about my dad? Is he involved with anyone? Has he remarried?"

I shook my head and told AJ that Mike thinks he's still married to your mom. I was glad AJ was still awake—I told him I wasn't sure what I would do alone in Albuquerque when Joe and his crew went home at the end of the week.

AJ put his arm around my shoulder. He said he had heard Joe ask God to protect me, as if I were his child. And that—he said, would make me his sister. If they leave you here—Big Brother will protect you.

I leaned my head against his arm, and said I like that. "But you've got some competition—cause everybody that works for Joe—treats me like a little sister." I didn't want to tell AJ that Joe suggested marriage before I lost my baby. AJ rubbed my arm briskly and said I'd be okay. He didn't think his dad would let anyone hurt me.

I wondered if Joe or my parents would allow me to work. Could I work, or would I be a burden for the rest of my life?

When I saw Doctor Burke, he asked what had happened to the feisty, spirited, and vivacious girl he had operated on just a few days before. He said he knew I was all those things, even though he was sure I was scared shitless. I didn't want to tell him that I was afraid I would disappear if I had to stay in Albuquerque and look at my feet when Joe's crew went home.

Doctor Burke touched my elbow and said, "I think you're ready for a road-trip." He guided me to the elevators and out the front door. I heard Joe's truck when he put me into AJ's car with my mother. When we stopped and the engines were turned off—someone opened my door. I took a deep breath. I was home—or as close to home as I could be—at the rodeo. Mike helped me out of the car, and I asked if Smokey had missed me.

Mike hissed when he answered yesss but said I couldn't go to him now because the doctor's watching me. He took me to the fire ring and the crew made room for me. We talked and we laughed. There were stories to tell and I was a part of the conversation.

When everyone got quiet—Doctor Burke said, "Let me say that now, I understand you and the men you work with." I almost lifted my face to look at the doctor and he laughed. "Down the road you can go back to work. That is, if this motley crew will have you." There were chuckles from all around the circle and more than a few— Hell-yeses.

I held my breath and waited. I was sure there would be a "but."

Doctor Burke knelt in front of me and said he had seen Mike turn me away from the horses. "My guess is—that one of them is yours."

I nodded, afraid that I wouldn't be able to speak.

"I don't care how much your horse means to you. You can't go anywhere near an animal of that size for fear of them knocking into you." Doctor Burke reached out and touched my face. "Your sight depends upon it, no bumps, no bruises, no rough housing. You're going to have to live with a mountain of restrictions for the time being. In time, my rules will relax, but I'll tell you what you can do, when and where."

"If I accept that, do I have to stay in Albuquerque? Or can I go home with Mom, and get back to the ranch when this bubble thing is over?"

My surgeon was quick to answer. He squeezed my hands, "I'll see you back here in two—no—three weeks." Mom said we could do that. "No airplanes. Take time to get home and the same coming back."

I breathed a sigh of relief and then heard Mom say, "I am so sorry we're not staying longer." Alex told her not to worry. He said he was sure that this was the best news I could have gotten.

Mom stepped back, and George said, "Careful now. I'll drive you and Chris to Oklahoma." I don't think Mom expected to hear those words from anyone—certainly not George. "Boss says I drive Chris home, nobody else."

"That's not necessary," Mom said. "I realize why you or any of the others would want to drive her, but I can drive my own car."

Joe spoke up, "I'd prefer it if George drove. He will stay with Chris until you need to bring her back to see her doctors. He'll be your packer, your loader. Whatever you need him to do, he will do."

"Don't you trust me?" Mom asked.

Joe hesitated, "I trust you. I've trusted the doctors. Now I'm asking you to trust George. He's the only man I know who can get Chris home and back again safely to us."

Mom started to say something else—but I stopped her, "It's all right mom—he's a good driver."

"I'd rather not be without him," Joe said, "But if Chris leaves Albuquerque, George takes her."

"The doctors will have something to say about this," Mom said under her breath, and she approached Doctor Burke. He told my mother that Alex was taking him back to the hospital and that she should come along—he was giving me permission to stay at the rodeo grounds until she was ready to head for home. He said that if it weren't for their move to Silver City, he would allow me to return to the ranch. When my surgeon said George would drive mom's car, she was furious.

"I can drive my own car," she blurted out.

Doctor Burke spoke sternly as he reached out to my mother. "Mrs. Latham, it's about her eyes, not your driving. A change in elevation can cause pain and possible blindness."

George approached and he said, "Doc, I could make the drive in two days, but I think three might be better. My maps have elevation lines. If you approve and the gas bubble co-operates, I can make our stops every 200-foot drop or rise in elevation. Do you want a thirty-minute stabilizing pattern, or should the stops be a full hour?"

Everyone kissed the top of my head when they said goodbye to me. AJ had followed mom back to the fairgrounds and he kissed my cheek. When he stepped away from me, Joe took his place. "I'm going to miss you and all the trouble you brought with you in May." Joe held me tightly and pulled his blue bandana from his pocket when he helped me into the back seat of Mom's car.

George held his maps as he waited for my mom to get into the car. When he slid behind the steering wheel—he said we'd eat lunch at a truck stop he knew about. After that, we'll use back roads until we get inside the Oklahoma border.

Mom said we should do the interstate. George smiled when he told her—if we did that, we'd be spending a lot of time alongside the road—waiting for my bubble to settle down. He wanted to show us some sights and take some interesting detours to help pass the time when we had to stop for my eye.

Mom looked at the maps when George placed them on the seat and asked why is there an X through Cuervo? George never answered and I didn't say anything about what had happened there, but I thought she turned in her seat to look at me.

When we stopped for the first night, George held my hand as I got out of the car and I thanked him for driving. "Yes, thank you for de tours," Mom chimed in. "You were right. This was much more interesting than the interstate, and there was no reason to go through Cuervo." George squeezed my hand.

At midnight I realized mom had gotten out of bed and the door to our room was open. I could smell the clear mountain air. I went to the open door and heard George's voice, "I believe every star in the night sky represents the soul of someone who died. My mother's up there—somewhere," he said. "She died when I was born, and I believe she takes care of babies who were never given the chance to live. I haven't told Chris that—but maybe—maybe you can tell her that my mother is taking care of her baby."

I went back to bed and when mom came inside, she laid down beside me. I told her I was glad George was driving us home and she said, "Me too—me too."

Chapter 20

When we got home late on the third day, we saw that Dad had been busy. He had pulled boxes from the basement; they were all open and stacked—two boxes high around every chair. I emptied each box—one piece at a time. If I wanted to keep anything Mom had saved, I had to put it in a new box and label the box as mine. It didn't take me long to realize time would go by quickly.

Dad took George with him to rent a truck when we couldn't move around in the house. They didn't return for several hours, and Mom asked what had taken so long. Dad said George is an interesting man, and we had coffee.

George filled the truck before the movers came to empty the house. Mom turned over all the keys we had to the real estate people and we went back inside for one last look before we went to my father's grave. We were leaving the past and my father behind when we headed to Albuquerque that day.

We stopped at AJ's apartment, but he had already moved out. When we got to a motel, George called the ranch—Joe said Alex was on his way and George said we'll stop too—before I take the family over to Silver City. Once I unload the boxes for the doctor and the misses, I'll be home. We might have to keep the truck until you can add on to the house for all her stuff."

I yelled loud enough for Joe to hear me and George handed me the receiver. I told Joe to change my bedding so Alex would have a clean bed while he was there. I was sure the doctors weren't going to allow me to return to the ranch yet. They thought I was going to be in Oklahoma for three weeks, but it had only been a little over eight days, and including our drive time, it was two weeks. Besides that, I told Joe last May that if family came to visit—I'd stay elsewhere.

The doctors were delighted my retina was staying put the next day, but sad that I wasn't seeing any better than I was. There had been some improvement and eventually glasses would help—but I'd never drive again or read from my journals.

In Silver City, my parents had taken a hotel suite, but Mom was anxious to find a home. "I know you'll soon go back to Joe's where all your friends are. They're are all like big brothers to you, aren't they?" Mom didn't wait for an answer as she closed the door behind her.

"They are, except for Joe and Mike," I said softly.

"And they're different?" Dad looked over the empty coffee mug he held to his lips.

"I feel an extra closeness with them, and some of the others."

"Do you feel like talking? Your mother's looking at houses all afternoon."

I swallowed past the lump in my throat and asked Dad if he was sure. He suggested we walk over to see what his new office looked like. He left a note for Mom to call when she got back.

As we walked, I talked about the men I worked with—and how Mike's brother died this summer.

"That's sad, did he work for Joe? Did you know him?"

"Sort of, but not very well, Mike and his brother were disconnected."

"Do you know why, and for how long?" As a psychiatrist—Dad asked questions and then he'd listen. I had grown up with questions. There always seemed to be a reason for them.

It was years ago, I said as we walked through the hospital entrance. I relied on Dad to guide me through the halls. "His brother was gay," I said quietly. "Mike had problems with that."

"Did he have a partner?" Dad asked as he stopped at a desk near his office, "If my wife calls, please let me know."

"Yes, Doctor, and if there are other calls?" the nurse on duty asked.

"I'm not scheduled, and my daughter's leaving soon."

"If somebody needs you Dad," I touched his arm. "They can interrupt."

"I'll interrupt if it's an emergency. Doctor, there's a water cooler in your office, but I could bring you coffee."

"Coffee please, black—no sugar, Chris is my water girl."

In Dad's office, he told me there was a couch. "Or," he said, "I can sit at my desk, and you could sit across from me. The chairs look comfortable."

I asked where's the couch and I claimed one of the corners. Dad filled a cup with water and gave it to me. I felt a coffee stir stick and smiled. He turned around a chair that faced his desk and then stood in the doorway to wait on his coffee, "Did James have a partner to share his life with?" Dad always remembered where he was in a conversation—but this time I had not called Mike's brother by name.

"I don't know for sure," I said as I bit my lower lip. "When James got really—really sick—the hospital called for Mike, but he wouldn't go to his brother."

"Did Mike ever reconnect with him?"

I turned to his voice. "In the middle of the night Joe took Mike to him. George was already at the hospital and all three were with James when he died."

Dad said thank you as he closed his office door and sipped at his coffee. "Sorry about the interruption. Let's get back to Mike and his brother."

"I think Joe was more a brother to both of them than they were to each other."

"What makes you say that?" Dad sat down and reached for a blank folder on his desk. He uncapped his pen and began writing. I asked if he was taking notes. "Yes dear, you know that I always do."

"Did Mike say anything to you?"

"I wasn't in Albuquerque long enough to talk with any of your friends. Do you think I should talk with Mike about his brother?" I thought for a minute and said it wouldn't hurt. Then Dad talked about Joe and Alex. "I was glad to see Alex with his father last week. They were separated for a long time."

"Really Dad," I took a deep breath and asked how they could be separated—when they were never together. When Dad asked about

Joe's wife—I shook my head. How could two people be married—and not know they made a baby? She never told Joe they had a son. How could anybody not know, and then I remembered.

Dad put the cap on his pen, and he walked around the coffee table to sit beside me. He reminded me of the circumstances surrounding my own conception and birth. I knew the story, but Dad told me again how he had grown up with his brother Geoff and the two boys often fought over who would take my mother to movies and dances. She had a tough time deciding between the brothers—but Geoff had won her heart. They married just after high school and mom followed him on the rodeo circuit that summer. In the fall he was drafted, and my mother began her studies to become a teacher while he was gone. In the late spring all three met to celebrate my parents' anniversary. Gregg said that if anything happened in Korea—he would take care of Helen.

Gregg was true to his word and married my mother in July. Mom had changed her name once, and she didn't have to do it again—Gregg and Geoff had the same father, just different mothers. In August they learned Mom was pregnant—and when I was born in December—they put Geoff's name on my birth certificate.

I asked Dad why they never had a child together and he took a handkerchief from his pocket. Perfectly pressed and creased, he wiped tears from his eyes, "Believe me Chris—when I say we tried—but it wasn't meant to be. Don't feel sad for me—because your father allowed me to be your dad and then Jennifer's family moved next door. When the two of you played, all four of us felt as if we had given each of you a sister.

Mom called to say she would pick us up because she had found a house we might like to see.

When my parents brought me back to the ranch, I told Dad he should read the journal I left behind in his desk drawer. He smiled and said that's a good place to start and then we can talk.

Chapter 21

At 1:55 I left the house with my walking stick; Joe and the crew were due back at two. I walked off the porch and went straight until I reached the fence. With it to my left, I walked to the road. It wasn't long before I heard engines; the sound would change as each vehicle reached the flat just before Joe's drive. One at a time the air horns sounded, the third rig stopped and idled in the drive. Joe asked if something was wrong when he came to my side.

When I said I was just waiting for him to get home—Joe took my free hand and guided it to the cab's vertical rail. I climbed into the rig and straddled the shifting mechanism. I told Joe that I wanted to go to the rodeo at the end of the week, but he said not before I saw my doctors.

Dr. Burke said I could ride Smokey each day, but I still had to wait to practice barrels. I knew that when he said I was ready, I only had to lean forward and yell "hup," before we would be on our way.

At the next rodeo Joe and I didn't go down to the dance. We could hear the band playing from our campfire. I asked how often he and Dad discussed me. Joe reached out and touched my kneecap. "I think you know better than that. I talk with Gregg because I need to. We listen to each other—yes—we talk about what happened and how it affects us—but we don't talk about you." I accepted what he told me as the truth.

While I had been gone Joe hired a young man who didn't know a whole lot about anything. I went to bed after saying I hope Mike's keeping him out of trouble. But before I fell asleep Mike brought Danny back from town and I listened to both men question him about what he wanted to do with his life.

In the morning Joe took him to breakfast and I asked Mike if he knew what Dan's problem was—he said he's gay. I asked if he was gonna try to change him. Get him to make the right choice? Mike shook his head, "The kid doesn't have a choice, any more than James did, or George does. And you need to talk about what happened to you."

I knew Mike was right and I nodded my head. Most of the men I worked with would listen—if I ever felt like talking, but I never felt pressured. I tried soo hard not to think about what happened in Cuervo because it made me sick when I did. *I never wanted to go back.*

Mike spent a lot of time with Dan. I heard Joe tell them once— that the time would come when homosexuals could be open about their beliefs, but in the seventies—Mike said Danny shouldn't be advertising what he was. Eventually—Dan asked if Mike would help him explain things to his family and he went back home.

After Dan left, I asked Joe why he hired us—meaning myself, Tom, and I don't know how many others. "Why don't you just put an ad in the paper?"

Joe answered simply and succinctly, "You needed jobs. You all worked out. I don't see a problem." He placed his hand on my back and said he hired people that some might not. "But all of you just happened to be in the right place at the right time." He smiled and I shook my head as I walked away. *Some things just didn't make sense to me.*

That same day—George watched Snowball show interest in an un-bred mare. I had grown accustomed to breeding discussions around the breakfast table—and Joe wanted the mare to foal the next year. I walked over to George and asked if he and James were together a long time. George looked at me and then back to Snowball, "What do you want to know?"

I took a deep breath and asked, how do you make it?

George didn't even turn around to ask, "What are you asking me?"

I wasn't sure why I was asking about two men—when I really wanted to know why the rapist did what he did to me. I asked George how he made love to James.

119

George nodded and I thought he was going to ask me to explain in detail what I wanted to know. He said Snowball just filled the uterus of that mare with his sperm and there will be a foal next summer. That's not love—it's procreation—and we watched the deed be done. George ignored the horses and turned to see my face. "I loved James and what we did with each other—how we conveyed our love—was the right thing for us and we kept it private. Loving James was something personal. I hope you understand." George was silent for a moment, "No matter who it is you fall in love with—you'll find what works for the two of you. As men, we are different from women, just as horses are different from us." George reached out to pinch my cheek and I grinned. "We could pleasure each other, as a man can pleasure himself."

I didn't realize what I was asking when I said, "But how?"

George sighed and he was brutally honest. There had been sex ed in school, but today I thought George would have been a better teacher. He asked if the rapist made me go down and I turned away— I didn't want him to see me cry, but I told him everything.

The next week Dad came to the ranch without my mother—he returned my journal. He said he was disappointed and had seen where I removed several pages. I went to my room and searched beneath my mattress. When I couldn't find the pages, I went to stand in front of Joe's desk. He looked up and asked, "what's wrong," when I didn't say anything.

I asked if Joe took journal pages from my room. He opened the center drawer of his desk and I kept talking. "What did you do with them? Nobody has the right to read them but me! And you know that."

Joe picked up an envelope. I could see that something was written on it and I asked what it said. "It says we didn't read anything. That means we didn't read what I put inside that envelope."

"Are these my journal pages? And who do you mean when you say 'WE'?"

Dad came to stand behind me, and Joe cleared his throat. "When Alex came from Albuquerque, we flipped your mattress, and these pages ended up on the floor."

"Have you known this whole time—what I wrote in my journal? Does Alex know too?"

I took the envelope from Joe and my hand touched his. "Alex said I shouldn't read your pages but should return them to you privately."

"You didn't do that," Dad's hands tightened on my shoulders and *the panic I had felt when I couldn't find the pages disappeared.* "Why didn't you just put them back?"

"That would have been wrong. I thought someone should be with you—when you were ready to talk about what you wrote down."

I thought about George and everything I had told him as I opened the envelope. I looked at the words I had written, but I couldn't read my own handwriting. I took a deep breath and placed the pages flat on Joe's desk. "I know what I wrote down in my journal and what I didn't. I talked to George and told him what happened because I thought he would answer questions—and not judge me." I drew in a deep breath and stepped away from both men. "If I must tell someone else what happened to me—I will. But let me decide when and who I'll tell."

Dad stayed for lunch and half of Joe's crew went back to work after eating. The table was cleared, and several conversations took place in the kitchen while the dishes were washed and put away.

George sat at the other end of the table and my eyes focused on his face—I could see him nod his head ever so slightly. Without demanding anyone's attention—I began to talk. Conversations stopped and Tom, John—Joe, Mike and my dad sat back down. I talked about what happened in Cuervo. I said John's sister had saved my life—because John recognized what had happened to her—was happening to me that day.

No one asked me any questions and I said that I had tried to be brave—but felt stupid. Dad assured me that I was courageous, and I would be okay because I had people around me who cared and would listen to me.

Over the holidays Mom gave me cigar boxes filled with day sheets and belt buckles. They belonged to my father and Joe said he might have met him. I put the boxes on the shelf with my journals.

Chapter 22

Mother's Day was Sunday, and we headed back to Santa Rosa. Joe rode beside me Friday night as I carried the National flag for the Grand Entry. He signaled to the announcer that I would represent him at the introductions. He took the flag from me and rested the pole on the top of his boot as I rode out to face the grandstand filled with people. I positioned my hat on my head when we were finished. In the dark Joe placed the flag's pole in my boot cup. The spotlight was on the flag, and I grabbed the pole—shaking out the flag, I spurred Smokey to jump. I heard his hooves beneath me, and the flag whipped above me as we circled the arena in darkness.

Once outside the arena Joe said I made some fancy moves during the introductions. Mike chimed in and called me "Fancy Clancy." I smiled thinking that this is the life my father wanted.

The sheriff rode up behind us and asked, "Whatever became of that youngster you hired last summer?"

I turned to him and said, "I'm back," and I grinned. When it was time for the barrel race, Mike waited for me at the gate. Joe said to be careful and the Sheriff asked if I was the favorite this year.

"You could say that," Joe told him. "Legally blind, she has competed since January and hopes to make the finals."

"Blind?" the Sheriff asked. "What happened?" I turned to the two men and shook my head.

Joe said, "Legally. She still has some sight, although it's been quite a year for her."

I checked my stirrups and backed Smokey into a corner of the box. I leaned forward and dropped the reins on Smokey's neck. I let out my war whoop and all eyes in the arena followed me. I was racing against every other time that night. We passed the judge and circled the first barrel. Smokey headed for the second just as the bull Crazy Eight got so restless that his leg broke the bottom board of his enclosure. The bull continued to fight his way out of the confining space. He succeeded just as we circled the third barrel and headed for the gate.

The bull stood motionless in the arena. The cowboys on the fence watched—they realized how dangerous the situation could turn—and turn quickly. Joe and the Sheriff waited, and the judge's flag dropped. Mike had the gate open for us, and he pushed it shut when we were outside.

I turned in my saddle, and listened to the announcer say, for five long seconds, Crazy Eight was loose in the arena. He kept talking about the stock while Joe took care of his bull. Mike went back to the chutes and George took Smokey to cool him down. The Sheriff dismounted beside me, and we laughed about how a whole year had passed and some things still stayed the same.

Chapter 23

The following week, Grace wanted to draw blood one last time to be sure I wasn't carrying a sexually transmitted disease. She said, after this length of time I wouldn't have to worry about the rape ever again. When she called to say, "All was well," Mike said we should grill steaks and make our own ice cream.

Joe said I should wear one of the fancy dresses he had hung in my closet last fall—if I'd like to go out to dinner for a quiet celebration.

I looked from one to the other and said, "Let's do both." We had our cookout and cranked two freezers of ice cream.

Joe made reservations for just the two of us and I couldn't decide which dress I wanted to wear. Gram came to the house and helped me try on the dresses. I had bought a short black satin dress with a plunging neckline because it made me look older than I was. Gram wouldn't tell me what she thought when she hung it in the back of my closet. The second dress I tried on was peach in color. I liked the feel because it was velvet, but it was a winter formal.

I had one more dress to try on when Joe knocked at my door. Gram told him to go sit down, that I'd soon be ready. "That's the one you should wear," she said as she walked around me. Gram touched my hair. In the year I'd worked for Joe, it had grown quickly, and now she made sure all the curls were in place. She stopped in front of me and slipped her fingers inside my dress. I swallowed the spit in my mouth. Gram had shown Pamela techniques of dressmaking to make a woman look good, and I had learned to stand quietly for them both. From her pocket, Gram took a single strand of pearls and placed them around my neck.

"Joe just gets younger every day you're here." Gram kissed my cheek, took my hand, and led me into the living room. She stood back to watch Joe's face when I stepped into his line of sight. I turned a pirouette so Joe could see me in all my finery. My dress was long, the bodice fitted at my waist, with buttons from my shoulder blades down the middle of my back to the tip of my tailbone. Little cap sleeves were just off my shoulders. The pink satin skirt with soft gathers at my hips was full. As I moved, I could hear the fabric swish.

"My God, you are radiant," Joe said as I stopped to stand in front of him.

"Are you sure I look okay?" I carried a beaded purse to match the shoes that peeked from beneath the hem of my dress.

"You're gorgeous." Mike said from the kitchen and I heard whistles from behind him.

Reaching out, Joe took my hand in his. Gram and all the men I worked with watched Joe steady my elbow as I lifted my skirt to step into the truck.

After eating, Joe reached across the table and touched my hand. He tried to tell me that this was the first time he'd been alone with a woman in a very long time. I told him we'd been alone dozens of times. "But this is different," he said when a single dessert was placed in front of us with tiny forks. "I was young when I married Laurie and a part of me wants her to come home."

I studied Joe's face—maybe he was still in love with his wife. *I'd never seen him show any interest in a woman and* I asked about Laurie. Joe said they were wrong to marry so young. I said my parents got married the day they graduated high school.

Joe shook his head, "We weren't that young."

I said they had grown up together and he said he didn't know Laurie that well.

I told Joe this felt like a date and I asked if he would expect a kiss when he took me home. Joe said he didn't think it would be appropriate to kiss me when we left the restaurant.

I asked why not—and when we reached Joe's truck, he said, "I was young back then—and now—I know better. We should never have married or done some of the things we did." I remembered the rapist forcing himself on me and I turned away. Joe pulled a handkerchief from his pocket and lifted my glasses so he could catch a tear from my eyes. "You have nothing to be ashamed of. You were forced to do things you shouldn't have been asked to do."

When we got home, Joe parked the truck and said he wouldn't be kissing me at the front door. I released my seatbelt and turned to face Joe. "What do you mean—there's not going to be a goodnight kiss?' An 'I had a wonderful time kiss?' Or even an 'I'd like to do this again kind of a kiss!'" I asked, "What would be wrong with a kiss? I think a kiss would be nice."

Joe came around to open my door and he said, "But I'm not a young man. To kiss you would be wrong because kisses can take you—where you're not prepared to go."

I shook my head and told Joe that if he didn't kiss me—I would kiss him. Joe looked at me and said I believe you would. I reached out to touch Joe's face and I felt creases at the corners of his mouth and eyes. He was smiling—and now I did too. "That's better and I will kiss you," I said getting out of the truck. When I had both feet on the ground, I straightened my dress and placed my hand on his. At our front door, I told Joe, "I had a great time." I touched his face again and said, "I don't see an old man in front of me, just a kind man I'd like to kiss. Joe raised his hands to touch my face. His fingertips were soft and his nails—filed smooth. He had gotten more than a shave and haircut that morning.

I remembered learning how to kiss when I was only sixteen. We were two awkward teens, and we laughed and tried more than once to learn what to do with our tongues, and then Jen and I would compare notes. Tonight, I didn't think of Joe as an older man as his hands guided my lips to his. I kissed the man we all called Boss. There was an intimacy as Joe's tongue and my lips touched. I felt Joe's body against mine. Something hard pushed against me. My whole body shook as I stepped away from Joe, "Please don't hurt me.

"I'm sorry—I didn't mean to frighten you." Joe reached out to me.

"Please," I said again, as I took another step backwards. "Don't touch me."

Joe dropped his hands to his side, "I knew this was wrong." We stood facing each other at the front door. "Tell me what I can do to make this right with you?"

I didn't know what to say—Moments before I had eagerly kissed Joe—and *I didn't think we'd done anything wrong.* Finally, I said that I needed to get out of my dress.

Joe walked me to my room, and I asked for his help with the buttons down the middle of my back. Joe stepped into my room and stood behind me. I felt his fingers touch my neck and move down my back as he undid the little round buttons. My dress began to slip off my shoulders. My sleeves were at my elbows when he finished with the last button. My back and my shoulders were bare as Joe reached around me and his hands pressed my dress back against my body. He held my breasts in his hands and when I heard the door to my room close—I realized my dress had fallen to the floor. I stood in my room with just the string of pearls at my neck and stockings on my legs.

I pulled a flannel shirt from the hook on my door. I placed my dress on my bed and replaced my stockings with socks. When I had jeans and boots on—I opened my door and looked across the hall. As I buttoned my shirt, I remembered my demands of Joe the year before. When Mike's brother was dying, I had read notes in a folder left open on Joe's desk. Tonight—I wondered if Joe would write down how we had kissed or that he had seen me naked and touched my body. Did he know that I had felt something powerful consume me when we kissed—*Is that what he meant when he said to kiss would be wrong?*

When Joe came out of his room, he had changed into his everyday working clothes too. He apologized for taking so long to unbutton all my buttons as he snapped the cuffs of his shirt. He said he had closed his eyes, when he realized I didn't have a slip or camisole under my dress. *I wasn't wearing anything under my shirt now,* and he didn't say anything about holding my dress against my body. We faced each other in silence and then he asked if I would take a walk with him.

We left the house and when Joe opened the gate into the field, he said, "I'm sorry you felt threatened by me." Joe touched my cheek and pushed my collar aside to touch the pearls still around my neck. He said kissing the way we did—aroused him more than he expected it to. I felt his fingertips move down my breastbone, separating my shirt until they stopped between my breasts when he reached a closed button. Joe took my hand in his and we walked into the field.

I asked if he would write down everything that I did in a folder with my name on it? Will you write about kissing me, and touching me—and about your feelings? And then will you share everything that you write down with my dad?"

Joe released my hand and he faced me. "Why do you think I would write these things down? And why would I tell your dad what I did. I was wrong to kiss a girl your age. I know better."

I reached my fingers out to touch his lips. *I wanted him to stop talking so I could say he was mistaken about being wrong.* "You left the door to your office open when you took Mike to his brother. I saw a folder on your desk with my name on it. And you wrote down really personal stuff about me."

Joe breathed in deeply and said, "I did that because I wanted to help. I thought that if I wrote things down—I'd be able to figure out how to help you. I do that for everybody—I even have a folder for myself. I could show it to you back at the house."

"Isn't that something personal—like my journal—something that should be kept private?" I reached my hand out and touched Joe's arm.

Joe's hand covered mine as he continued, "It is personal, but you are kind and I don't think you would judge my thoughts and feelings—too harshly."

As I listened to Joe, I understood why he reminded me of my dad. I convinced myself that it would be wrong if I pursued a man his age—especially when I thought he was still in love with his wife.

We did return to Cuervo and we took Officer Terry with us. I rode with him when he drove one of Joe's trucks home. I told Terry—I wished someone like him had been there the night I was raped. Terry looked at me and then he told me what had happened to him. He said he was only twelve years old when he had been abused.

Terry asked if he could call on me for help—if someone were ever in the same situation, I had been in. I said yes and prayed that he would never make that call.

I never went on another date with Joe, or anyone else. We were busy with rodeos and there were dances every week and all of us would go. Everyone treated me like I was their little sister.

Some weeks we would work one rodeo, and George would take Smokey and I down the road still further so I could ride again. Mike always said that if I wanted to make Oklahoma, it was what I needed to do.

Chapter 24

On my second Thanksgiving, Joe planned a children's rodeo for Thursday and invited neighbors. My parents had arrived on Wednesday, and Mom enjoyed watching the men prepare for our dinner and the kids.

On Thursday, Mom came outside and found Joe talking with Dad. She interrupted them to say she had taken a call asking Joe not to detain Alex at the ranch for too long.

I asked if Joe thought Laurie was with Alex, and then Mike's whistle got my attention. Smokey snorted and pushed me toward the sound. Okay, okay, I'm going, I told my horse.

Mom laughed and called out after me, "That's the biggest guide dog I've ever seen."

"I like you too," I reached my hand back and gave Smokey's neck a rub.

"Gregg, will you take a walk with me?" Joe asked as I walked away.

When Alex pulled into the drive Mike saw him, and we both moved to the U-Haul's open window. Mike asked about his empty tow-bar.

"A friend has my car," Alex said as his truck idled.

"You mean your mom, don't you? I think she called and asked Joe not to detain you too long."

"I'm sorry about that. She was just supposed to drive around the area. I didn't mean for anyone to find out she was here." Alex scanned the riders in the field, as my parents came to the truck. "I don't see Dad."

My dad pointed to the barn west of the house—indicating that Joe had gone there.

Mike said SHIT—and I—bull barn—Dad asked if there was a problem.

"I hope not," Mike said.

Alex put his vehicle in gear to drive back. Smokey moved away and I told AJ to be careful if he went inside.

Mike reminded us that there was supposed to be a medic and station wagon at the ranch in case one of the kids got hurt. "When they get here," he told my parents, "Send 'um to the barn." Mike pulled my foot from the stirrup. "I'm coming up," He took the reins and in one quick move, he jumped Smokey to a gallop. Dirt and snow sprayed from the horse's hooves.

Mike pulled Smokey to a stop and was on the ground as Alex tried to open the barn door. "Stay out 'til I know it's safe," Mike told him.

I dismounted, leaving the reins drop to the ground. I followed the sound of Mike's boots. Once inside the barn we waited for our eyes to adjust to the dim light and we heard Joe's voice, "It's hard to believe I pulled you out the day you were born." It sounded as if he were inside one of the pens. "I'd have given all this up to see my son become the man he is today." Alex listened to his father as we moved to Joe's voice. "How could Laurie be so cruel as to deny me time with my son?"

Alex called out, "Dad. I'm here."

Joe heard the words he had wanted to hear for years. He turned and realized that his trip down memory lane had taken him inside the stall with Crazy Eight. In that moment, the two men were frozen in time. The bull charged. AJ's eyes filled with terror. His fear was reflected to Joe. The bull's horns appeared from either side of Joe's body. The bull snorted, dropped his head and Joe's body rose into the air and like a beach ball bounced off the ground and came to rest in straw bedding. Crazy Eight turned. His right hoof went through the crown of Joe's hat. The brim remained on the bull's leg, and the bull fixated on it.

Alex dropped to his knees and reached between the boards of the gate to his father's twisted body. "Dad, can you hear me?" Half of

Joe's face was buried in straw. Alex watched the bull eye the hat's brim on his leg.

"Stay out," Joe whispered. "It's better this way."

"That's not happening." Alex stood and looked for a second access into the cubicle. Mike had already moved off to my left through an aisle too narrow for any of the bulls to get through. He headed for that second entrance into the stall. Alex climbed the gate and saw the passage from above. The entire barn was laid out with each box stall having a front and back door.

Mike worked the latch and opened the gate into the aisle. Joe's hat was now in the bull's mouth and neither had anything to prod the animal to move out of the stall.

"You bastard, get the hell out of here." Alex startled himself as he dropped into the stall and moved to the bull. Mike was waving his arms to draw the bulls' attention to him and the open gate. Crazy Eight lowered his head and went through the opening. Mike slithered into the stall and together they pulled the gate shut and secured it. They were safe, but in a cell guarded by a 2000-pound animal and blocked by Joe's body. Alex knelt beside his father, pushing straw away from his face. "You're safe now," he said, his hand resting in the dirt. Joe still had not moved. "I'm sorry—this is all my fault."

I climbed into the enclosure when Mike dropped to his knees. "Did he step on you?" I heard Mike ask as he checked for a pulse. Joe groaned and I lunged for him. AJ grabbed hold of me, and I screamed for him to let go.

"Stay back. I mean it, Chris!" Mike's face was in the dirt when Joe said his life was over. Mike said hell no, as he reached for my hand. "I don't know how badly he's been hurt—talk to him—Don't try to touch or move him."

"You know the rules," I told Joe as more help came into the barn with Dad in the lead. Alex pulled me away so the medic could get close. A neck collar and backboard were passed over the fence. With the collar around Joe's neck, four men carefully moved him onto the backboard, and he was carried out of the stall.

"It's a hard and fast rule that *nobody* comes into this barn alone," Mike said.

My dad spoke up, "Joe said he could break his own rules."

Mike shook his head, "If I couldn't move—that would be reason enough to end my life. But Joe's better than me." AJ was still holding me back when Mike looked at me, "He's got a lot to live for." Mike told the driver to get on the road and then asked my dad to take AJ and I into town. He said he'd call to let Grace know what had happened before he left the ranch.

At the clinic Alex asked if his mother had caused this. Joe said "No, this was just an axe-i-dent, pure and simple. Alex—I turned when you called out. I wasn't paying attention and I got hit, but I behaved. I haven't tried to move."

Doc stood in front of Joe when Joe asked him to wrap his ribs. "I wish you cowboys would leave the doctoring to the doctor." He took the x-rays from his wife's hand and held them to the overhead light. "Let's get you wrapped up and shipped out with a bow. We've got dinners to eat and I like mine hot."

Joe rested his arms on Doc's shoulders while his chest was wrapped. Doc wasn't a tall man and yet his voice carried to all in the room. "Neither lung has been punctured, but he needs to be watched, and his breathing monitored." He paused to look up to Joe's face. "You've broken eight true ribs, the ones that attach themselves to the backbone and sternum."

Joe had planned dinner at two. It was almost that when we returned from town. Gram fixed a plate of food, and she took a glass of water to Joe's room. A spoon was the only utensil she wanted, and she said a towel would work better than a paper napkin.

After dinner was over, most drifted to the television and football. Alex asked if Joe needed help to the bathroom and I said, "Don't make him get up." I left the room to run a basin of hot water. I set out soap and a towel. I pulled the porcelain urinal from under the sink and Alex helped me to carry everything to Joe's room.

When the phone rang, Dad moved through an opening in Joe's bedroom to his private office to answer the phone. He stepped back into the opening to see Joe attempt to use the urinal and told Alex to help his father.

I moved to Dad's side as he waited for the caller to speak and I reminded him that AJ's mother had spoken to Mom.

"Are you still on the line?" Dad moved out of Joe's sight. "I'm Chris Latham's father—I'm visiting her for the holiday—did Alex tell you about my daughter?"

Dad held the receiver so I could hear and finally, I heard a woman ask if she could speak with Joe Engelmann. Dad proceeded carefully. He said Joe was resting after a slight mishap that morning. "His son is with him, but Alex hasn't said how long he expects to stay. Do you know?"

"We had plans for three o'clock today. Let me find a room for the night. We can leave in the morning."

I went to Joe's side and told Alex he didn't have to leave until morning. He took the urinal with him when he went to my dad and took the phone from him.

I tried to straighten Joe's covers, but he pushed my hands and the blanket off his chest.

I heard Alex tell his mother to stay away. He said he'd find her when he was ready to leave, not before. When Alex returned, he placed the clean urinal under Joe's bed, and I left them alone to talk. Dad was still holding the receiver, and I touched his arm to get his attention. "There's no place for her to stay." Dad asked what he should tell the woman—should she come to Joe's?

"Alex doesn't want me there—it's bad enough I'm in town."

I took the receiver and told her to come. I'm sure Gram has a spare room and you should talk to Joe. When mom took Gram home, they both told us not to say anything about Joe's wife.

Mom was gone for hours and when she returned, she went straight to Joe's room. "Help your father with the urinal," she told AJ. "It's late and we all need some sleep." She asked me for several park blankets—saying that if we rolled them into two tubes, we could put them on either side of Joe, and the weight of his covers wouldn't put any pressure on his fractured ribs.

Alex had gone to the kitchen and was talking with Mike. I told my parents to use my bed since I invited Laurie to stay at Gram's. I intended to sit at Joe's side all night.

When we had the blanket rolls in place and the covers up to Joe's neck, Dad came to see what we'd been doing. "Now let the man, get some sleep," he said.

It was only ten o'clock, but the whole house was quiet. At eleven, I felt a chill and went over to open the fireplace damper. I found matches and ignited the kindling, the limb wood was dry, and it didn't take long to catch fire. When the logs were burning, I went back to Joe's side. His bed was huge, and he wasn't using much of it. I was exhausted and I needed to sleep, so I picked up an extra blanket and laid down with it beside Joe.

At midnight, Alex was standing over me. "What do you think you're doing?" He said as he pulled me off Joe's bed and the blanket covering me fell to the floor. The light in the hall was on and Alex saw that I was fully dressed. The rolled blankets were still in place—Joe and his bedding had not been disturbed.

"What's wrong?" Joe asked, lifting his head.

I disentangled myself from Alex and placed my hands, on Joe's shoulders, "Shush now, don't try to get up. I'm not going anywhere." I kissed his cheek and lay down beside him again.

Alex bent over to pick up my blanket. He covered me and whispered in my ear, "I guess you didn't do anything wrong." He spent the rest of the night sleeping in the chair beside Joe's bed.

In the morning Joe tried to tell me we would leave for the last rodeos of the year as soon as Alex got on the road. I thought about the crowds and the rush to make the next performance, but I shook my head. "If I make the finals, so be it. But I'm not leaving you like this and you're **NOT** going anywhere."

When Joe said we were going, I yelled NO, and I woke Alex. "Your body needs time to heal."

It will, Joe said. "Mike can drive, and I'll only leave my bed long enough to see you ride."

I stomped my foot. "We're not going anywhere, Joe." Alex folded the blanket I'd left on the chair.

"What's wrong?" Dad asked as he and my mother appeared in the doorway.

"Chris has done so well, but she needs a few more buckles and prize money to secure her spot at the finals."

"Let's not get ahead of ourselves," Dad said. "We've got personal business to attend to before anybody leaves the house." He sent Mom and me to the kitchen, saying that he and Alex would help Joe.

When Alex got to the kitchen, he seemed nervous. The phone rang and he was called to the receiver. "I can't do this here," and he bolted out of the room. Mom went after AJ and he asked, "Why couldn't she just stay home?"

"She's your mother," Mom answered. "She loves you—and your father. Go over there and bring your mother back." Mom stood at the open door and watched Laurie take her son into the little house across the field.

"I'll get Joe his breakfast and when Alex brings his mother, they need to talk. Mom left the room without another word.

When AJ returned with his mother, I reached out and took Laurie's hand, "Joe's waited a long time for you to come home." Laurie's hesitated at the open door of Joe's room. My mother had just straightened Joe's bedding and she asked me to come to the kitchen when she picked up Joe's breakfast tray.

"In a minute," I said as I pulled at Laurie's hand. Alex left with my mom—and I told Joe, "There's someone here to see you." Joe opened his eyes and asked if he had died and gone to heaven.

Words and feelings—that had been kept inside for years—spilled from Laurie's lips. "After making love to you I did not know—When I left, I didn't know—When the lawyer sent divorce papers I still did not know, and when you returned them—it was too late to come home. I was sure that if anything happened and I lost your child—you'd blame me."

"Is that why you left me alone—without saying a word?"

"I thought it was best that you never knew I tried to have your baby."

"But AJ was born, and Joe suspected you were pregnant," I told her.

"I know that now. I just didn't know if I could carry a child to term when I got pregnant. Joe knew that there was one pregnancy that ended." Laurie reached out and touched Joe's hand, "I couldn't bear the thought of your doubts and suspicions if anything happened.

"You had no faith in me—no faith that I would understand and grieve the loss of our child if it came to that?"

Mom had come back with Alex to stand in the doorway of Joe's room. She said Laurie showed Alex the buckle, "The one that led your son to find you."

Laurie turned to look at her son, "I hoped, but never allowed myself to imagine that you would find your father." Laurie leaned over Joe, "Will you ever forgive me—for leaving the way I did?"

Joe reached out to touch her face as Mike came to stand beside me.

"I would have understood," Joe said as Mike squeezed my hand tightly.

I held my breath and heard Mike say, "Let's get you out of here—now." He led me through the same door he had carried me through—when I lost my baby.

Joe said he never stopped waiting for Laurie to come home.

Mike watched Laurie remove the rings she wore. She kissed them and placed them in Joe's hand, closing his fingers around them. Mike said we shouldn't be listening to this—just as my mom came outside with us. I heard Laurie say, "It should be your decision—not mine as to who wears your mother's diamond." Mom pulled the house door shut.

On the porch, outside Joe's room, Mike said she had chosen to leave, but none of us knew why. Mom touched my hand and said, "We understand—don't we?"

Alex found me backing from the stall in the new camper. He pulled a chain from his neck to expose two bands of gold and a diamond ring. "Dad wants me to keep these until I find the right girl."

I snapped the rope behind Smokey. "Is there a girl?" I asked as Alex lifted the ramp and bolted it shut.

"God, I love you," Alex cried out as he turned to face me. "But I don't think Dad would approve. He'd tell me not to get involved with my sister—but maybe you have a friend you could introduce me to." *I looked at AJ and thought he would like Jennifer. I wondered if he had any idea, I had been pregnant, and that Joe was with me when my baby died.*

Mike brought Laurie to say goodbye. She asked us to take care of Joe and Mike said we would. He grabbed my hand and held it up between us and said we always will. He said we'd take care of Alex too.

I was glad Laurie had come with her son. After all the years—I thought Joe deserved to know why she left.

Chapter 25

I stopped in the hall and listened to Joe say, "If I do nothing else in my life, I need to explain to my son why Laurie felt the need to leave."

"What is there to explain?" Dad leaned in close to listen.

"I'm afraid that I judged her—or she felt as if I would—if she couldn't bring a child into our marriage. If I hadn't been so self-centered, I might have seen Alex grow to be the man he is today."

I went into Joe's room and I touched my stepfather's hand. He looked at me and I said, "I thank God every day—for allowing my uncle Gregg to be my father and my dad." I smiled, took a deep breath and then turned to face Joe, "I know you would have been a father to the child that died inside of me—because that's the kind of man you are. You didn't belittle me or accuse me of doing anything wrong. As a man you wanted to love a child—I think that's all you ever wanted."

I opened Joe's door to the outside as Dad, in his red flannel shirt helped Joe to his feet. Mike had placed a wide plank between the porch and the camper so Joe wouldn't have to go up or down steps. Dad helped Joe onto the first bed he came to, "I'll leave your boots, but don't get out of this bed."

"He won't, dear." My mother said as she appeared behind me with her arms full of blankets. "Not with the four of us to watch him."

George set my parents luggage inside the camper. I buckled myself in as he removed the loading plank. Mike pulled at the air horn when we turned onto the road. He hammered the gas pedal, and four hours later he spotted the truck Alex drove. Alex and his mother had stopped to eat, but there was still twenty miles to go before that afternoon's rodeo, and we'd be cutting it close.

Mike hurriedly backed Smokey from the trailer and saddled him for me. Inside the camper, Mom helped me to change shirts and we went down to the arena with Mike and Smokey. Dad brought Joe from the camper just before my name was called.

I had the chance for a few deep breaths before my run, and I earned third place. Joe said I would have another chance tonight. But I almost missed that, and Joe said second place was better, before he went back to his bed.

As much as Joe wanted to see me on ride Saturday, we convinced him not to leave the camper. Mom stayed with him, while Dad came with Mike and me. I earned another second that afternoon, and we moved on down the road to make an evening performance. That night I won my buckle by just a fraction of a second.

Dad said he'd take Smokey back to our camper if Mike and I would get us something to eat. We had eaten all the food we brought with us and the camper would stay parked for a few hours. Mike said there would be enough time to get to California if we left at four. Mike rolled off his bed at a quarter to four, and at four he was driving West—while the rest of us slept.

Alex caught up to us on Sunday and there was time to exercise Smokey before the grand entry. Joe insisted he was going to sit in the stands like a real spectator today. Mom said he'd not been at all comfortable with me out of his sight. "And now he's going to watch from the stands. You—be careful," Mom admonished me.

"I will but you have to keep him in the stands," I told her.

I sat on the fence with Mike. Joe and the others were in the middle of a row, halfway up in the grandstand. Mike said they had good seats to see everything, but I worried. I asked Mike if he knew why Laurie had left so many years before.

"I speculated about another man. Doc Williams came looking for her after she left, but he never said why. When Laurie returned Joe's rings yesterday, I got the sense that she truly loved him. I don't know if she even understands why she left."

I took Mike's hand in mine and said, "She knows, and Joe understands. All he has to do now—is to explain what happened, and why, to Alex."

142

"Joe just followed Alex out of the grandstand," Mike said, and he asked if I thought we should follow them.

I said lets just stay put and pray that Joe has the situation under control—and that he makes it back by the time I ride.

Mike said Joe would be back, and he was right. Joe stood between his son and Mike to watch as Smokey passed the judge, circled the first barrel, and headed for the second. I left the arena that day with two more buckles and Joe was finally satisfied.

I led Smokey into his stall and prepared his food and water for the drive home. Inside the camper—on the other side of the wall—I heard Dad ask if Joe's family was all right.

Joe said my son knows this wasn't his fault—but more importantly—I didn't want him to blame his mother. "Laurie sacrificed herself, so Alex never felt neglected, and now that he's on his own, I hope she'll find someone to share her life with."

"What about yourself?" Dad asked.

"I'm all right Gregg, I believe Chris and your wife have everything under control."

Chapter 26

George drove my parents' car to their home, where we picked him up. When we got back to the ranch, George and Mike took Joe inside to help him shower. I had barely gotten his bed ready when they brought Joe to his room clean shaven and buck naked.

Mike had towels on his shoulder, and he told me put them down to keep Joe's bedding dry. Joe grabbed one to cover himself when George came with a basin of hot water. Mike took the towel and worked it under his butt cheeks. "Nobody's asking you to do anything."

I stepped up to Joe's side and began to wash his arms and then his legs. The two men on either side of his bed dried him with the towels he laid on. I rinsed the cloth and wiped the bar of soap. Joe turned his head away when I reached between his legs. "I know you're a proud man, but you need help tonight." I touched Joe—and I felt him grow hard. Mike quietly sang about his ding-a-ling and Joe told him to shut up.

George took the cloth from my hands and said, "I tried to answer your questions, and explain what an orgasm is all about. How just a touch will take a man to the pinnacle of excitement—culminating in the release of his sperm. George's hand closed around mine and we stroked Joe until he became even harder. Joe cried out as he wet himself and me. "What you hold is not a weapon," George said when he released my hand and squeezed water from the washcloth—he wiped semen from Joe's body and dropped the cloth into the basin of water. He stated—you haven't done anything wrong.

I took the basin to the bathroom and poured the soapy water down the drain. I undressed and allowed warm water to cascade over my body. I moved back, out of the water and with a bar of soap—I covered myself in frothy soap suds. I lifted my face under the shower head and like a summer rain—droplets of warm water washed away all the soap scum. When I had dried myself, I put on one of my many night shirts. I had kept all the t-shirts from my travels, and I could wear a clean one each night.

I returned to Joe's room to find Mike holding all the towels. George turned off the overhead light as I went to Joe's side. He tried to send me to my room, and I told him someone must pay attention to your breathing. I crawled into bed with Joe—there were no blankets to separate us tonight as I laid next to him, under the down comforter. "I know you won't hurt me—because you're not a monster."

George said that's right, as he and Mike left Joe's room. They left us alone to unload and clean out the camper. I was sure Smokey would run in the field for a long time before he'd fall asleep.

I listened to Joe's breathing, and I heard him say, "I think that girl I hired. That girl—that I thought was a boy—has a lot more to teach me. Joe took my hand in his and said that I had grown into a woman— who will love a man with her whole self. I held my breath when Joe released my hand. He had reminded me how I could touch faces and know if someone was happy or sad. When Joe touched my body, I wondered if he knew I had reached my own climax.

The finals were coming up soon. Joe arranged for the stock and confirmed our housing. My parents drove to the ranch and rode Oklahoma with us. Alex would fly in from California. Laurie said she would see Alex for Christmas but wasn't sure if she would make the finals.

Chapter 27

The finals consisted of ten rodeos. Fifteen finalists in each event had ten chances to win a buckle and prize money, but there was only one chance to take the overall gold. And that buckle wouldn't be determined until the last rodeo. A second gold would be awarded for points and earnings throughout the year. Bob Mason had made sure Tina rode at the most lucrative rodeos and her winnings were far ahead of mine. Joe said that if even if she had "off days" in Oklahoma—she would take home the gold for monies earned. I finally understood why Joe had pushed me to compete after he'd been hurt. I needed the buckles and prize money to make the finals, because if I weren't there, I would have no chance of earing a gold buckle.

In Oklahoma, Joe asked if he could come with my parents and I to the cemetery. He wanted to see my father's grave, and he sent my parents and I off to my piano teacher's grave. As we approached her headstone, mom said a new grave had recently been opened. Dad said it must have been Jen's father who died, and he left word for Jennifer. He wanted her to know that we were in town for the finals and I was there to compete.

As I waited for the last rodeo of the year, I remembered the first night in Oklahoma. I was ready to ride at the mention of my name, but the announcer kept talking. He said I got the last position out there. It was a wonderful achievement, he said, because I rode blind.

I let out my war whoop, but it was more of a cry, I buried my face in Smokey's mane and no one saw my tears. We flew from barrel to barrel and I heard the crowd cheer when Smokey slowed. My run was good, not good enough for first, but it was for second. Joe waited at the tunnel for me and I demanded to know who had told the announcer I was blind. I had not used my white cane, that screamed I was visually impaired.

Joe said he'd speak to the announcer and that was the last mention of my nonexistent sight. Although, when my name was called—all work stopped behind the chutes and all eyes were on me. Ticket holders paid attention to my rides, and applause from the rodeo people was greater for me than anyone coming in first.

Jennifer was part of the drill team that carried flags that year—but with my vision, I didn't realize I passed by her on the first night.

Jen thought she recognized me, but the program said I lived in New Mexico. It wasn't until she received Dad's message that she knew for sure. When we saw each other—we hugged, and my parents guided us to a more private area where we could untangle the past few years.

Jen's father had sold their home and moved away after the accident. He was sick for a long time and now Jennifer wasn't sure where she would go. She had paid for her father's funeral with her tuition money. My parents had heard her tale of woe and they stepped up behind me. Dad put his hands on my shoulders and said I should worry about my buckle. "Let Mother and I take care of Jennifer."

I thought that if Joe hadn't said something at my father's grave— I'd have never found Jennifer. It was the same as what happened in Albuquerque—if I hadn't been there—AJ might never have found his father.

Saturday finally arrived. Cameras and lights were aimed everywhere. Alex said he came to cheer me on, but I think he was there to check on Joe. I introduced Alex to my best friend—I blundered and called Jennifer my sister—he laughed and asked if this was my way to keep them apart. I shook my head and said I share a bond with my best friend, as if she were my sister but it would be nice if she could be a part of my family forever.

Tonight, we all knew precisely how quickly we needed to ride. Tina was so far ahead of everyone in money for the year that there was no chance to beat her. Mike said that even if she came in first tonight, she wouldn't be able to knock me out of the all-around standings. I was calm as I waited in front of Smokey, his chin resting on my shoulder. The grand entry was on national television, and Joe insisted he ride. Jen's drill team was posting the colors and I thought I saw a camera flash when she yelled out my name as we rode by. When her duties were over, she waited with my parents and AJ.

I entered the arena and positioned my horse when the announcer called my name. I heard the word "Go" and the flag signaled the start of my time when it dropped. My hands allowed Smokey to have as much autonomy as he needed. We were around one barrel, a second and on to the third. The reins were loose on my horse's neck. I didn't try to control him.

As we neared the tunnel entrance Smokey veered—a photographer blocked his path and he ran beside the fence. Spectators were on their feet as the announcer screamed, there's your winner. Chris Latham has taken tonight's buckle along with the gold. The crowd chanted my name and grew even more unmanageable as Smokey circled the arena.

At the tunnel entrance that time—Mike reached for Smokey's bridal. Once we were out of the crowd's direct line of sight, the noise began to subside. The announcer continued to speak of my accomplishments. "What an achievement for the young lady who has ridden blind all year. She takes home the gold buckle as All-Around Champion." The crowd was so loud that I don't know if they heard him say, "Tina Mason takes home another gold for the season's top earnings.

In addition to all the cameras in the Colosseum, flash bulbs were going off too. Photographers were hoping to capture the photo that would be chosen over all the others—for the next year's program.

Joe told me not to get so upset as he rested his hand on my thigh. I didn't hear Joe when he said, "Smokey's yours. You've earned him along with your gold buckle." I was still whining about the announcer—so Mike used my reins to snap at my leg. The sting got my attention and Joe said, "Tonight's crowd was wild and crazy about you before they knew about your eyes."

I slid from my saddle and when I was on solid ground, Joe reached out to touch my face. He brushed away my tears and his fingers parted my hair into multiple strands. He knocked my hat to the ground. It had been months since our date—but not that long since I had slept beside him. That day in Oklahoma, Joe held my face in his hands—

and we kissed. Our bodies came together as one—I pushed myself against Joe and felt him pull me closer. A man focused the lens of his camera.

Joe reached into his pocket and dropped to one knee—there were flashes of light as Joe opened a small piece of cloth in his hand and slipped a ring onto my finger—more flashes of light. Joe proposed to me and our images were projected on coliseum screens. I heard the words, "This is the ring Geoff gave your mother," when he placed a diamond on my finger. When I said yes—Joe stood—he removed his hat and sent it sailing into the stands—and we kissed again. I heard hands clap and feet stomp—there were more flashes of light as his tongue played with mine—I could only imagine giving myself to him.

Rodeo—and ranch life—is hard work—it takes a toll on a person's body—male and female. As hard and rough—as his work is—Joe's gentleness—and his compassion for others—never waivers.

EPILOGUE

A pine tree from the upper pasture was marked this summer. A candy cane ribbon was tied just below its new growth. When the first heavy snow came in December we rode to the upper pasture and searched for the ribbon of red and white. The two-man crosscut saw was set—the children—two at a time, pushed and pulled, and pulled and pushed, until the tree's trunk was cut clean through. Carefully the tree was laid on the sled, secured into place, and brought to the house. When we had the tree in its stand, the children searched for and found a nest.

It took days to string the lights and after that Joe brings a carved wooden box to me and places it on a stool. It sat beside the fireplace during the year, and now the children gather round and wait patiently for me to open the box. Inside there are angels of fabric and thread—precious metals and wood that was hand carved; there were glass blown angels too—engraved and adorned with names and dates. I give angels to each of the children and watch as one by one Joe and his first-born son lift the little ones so they could place their angels near the treetop. There were angels for everyone who would and would not celebrate the holidays with us—Jen, AJ and all our children searched through other boxes to find their own special ornaments. It took a long time to hang them all, and I'm afraid that someday we won't be able to get a tree large enough—into the house.

Now—with only the tree lighting the room—I send the children off to the kitchen to bring a platter of cookies for Santa and Joe kisses me when they don't return. There were mugs of hot chocolate and warm cookies waiting for them.

George brings cookies and chocolate for Santa—but he waits—not wanting to interrupt us. He finally makes his presence known and sets the tray down as I step back from Joe.

The entire family is under one roof tonight and photos have been taken. Jen takes Joes youngest from my arms and with AJ holding their son—the boys are laid in the same crib. My parents and Laurie put the older children to bed.

I pause to remember—now that everyone has left the room—that I have no photographs from my travels. Words remind me of where I've been, the sights I've seen—and sensations felt when I traveled by bus.

Years have passed and the mantle is now full of photographs. Each frame is identified so that when I dust, I know whose photo I hold in my hand. The first one I remember receiving was of several photos arranged and layered—in a frame. There was a piece of cloth in Joe's hand with a diamond ring—there was our kiss in the tunnel and one capturing the instant I won my gold buckle. There was a Christmas tree and a cake with a bride and groom. I will always remember the Christmas Eve I married Joe Engelmann. Then twice my age—the age difference now—is not so great and I have learned so much.

Gram, the Grand Dam of this place has died, but there is a photograph of her holding our first child and grandchild, one in each arm. Alex and Joe were kneeling beside their first and second born sons. I stood behind Gram along with my parents and Jen. I told Mike and George to come and stand beside me—because everyone was truly a part of this family that day. Jen asked Laurie and her friend—the photographer—to join us for the photo. When the timer was set, Laurie's friend had just enough time kiss her cheek before the flash went off.

Discretely, Laurie's friend collected old and worn photos from each of us—one of my father in uniform—Mike's brother in costume—wedding photos of Joe's parents and Jen's. He even had a photo of Mike's parents and James and George when they were young men.

The canvas he created was large and resembles an oil painting. It hangs above the mantle and because of its size—I can make out all the faces looking down on us—if I take my time and concentrate.

I'm glad Laurie has moved past Joe with her friend. They come at least once a year, but they don't stay with us for very long. They have their own lives to live albeit far different from ours. They send us photographs we don't remember being taken.

I think about Jim Bob's words,
    the games Mike plays with names,
        and George's many lessons.

I remember those who have died
    and the children
        who were never meant to live.

I believe Gram has them now that they're older—
    she's telling them what to do
        and how to behave.

Tonight, Joe comes looking for me and takes my hand in his. We walk past all the sleeping children in their beds and Joe closes the door behind us at the end of the hall.